Alister Ross

The Distant Past

and other stories

WILLIAM TREVOR

poolbeg press

William Trevor was born in Mitchelstown, Co. Cork, in 1928 and educated at St. Columba's and Trinity College, Dublin. He was a sculptor before he turned to writing, but since his early novel, *The Old Boys* (1964), which gained him the Hawthornden Prize, he has had either a novel or a collection of short stories published almost every year and has won most of the major literary prizes, including the Allied Irish Banks Award for Services to Irish Literature. Widely acclaimed as one of the modern masters of the short story, he is also a highly successful TV playwright, using, as often as not, his own stories as the basis for his work in this medium.

Married, with two sons, he lives in Devon.

This book is one of a series devoted to the modern Irish short story. Ireland's contribution to the short story is world famous, but much of the best work both of the acknowledged masters and of the new hands is either out of print or has never been published in book form.

The aim of this series is to make that work generally available.

Contents

Page

Author's Note   5
A Choice of Butchers   7
Memories of Youghal   26
The Ballroom of Romance   39
The Distant Past   61
Death in Jerusalem   71
The Time of Year   90
Attracta   103
The Death of Peggy Morrissey   124
Miss Smith   135
The Forty-seventh Saturday   147
Mr McNamara   159

This collection first published 1979 by
Poolbeg Press Ltd.,
Knocksedan House,
Swords, Co. Dublin, Ireland.

These stories first appeared in: *The Eleventh Ghost Book, The Irish Press 'New Irish Writing', The New Yorker, Penguin Modern Short Stories, The Times, Transatlantic Review, Winter's Tales from Ireland.*

Miss Smith first published in volume form in "The Day We Got Drunk On Cake and other stories" © William Trevor 1967; *The Ballroom of Romance, The Forty-seventh Saturday,* and *A Choice of Butchers* first published in volume form in "The Ballroom Of Romance and other stories" © William Trevor 1972; *The Distant Past* and *Mr McNamara* first published in volume form in "Angels At The Ritz and other stories" © William Trevor 1975; *Death in Jerusalem* and *Attracta* first published in volume form in "Lovers Of Their Time and other stories" © William Trevor 1978.

The generous assistance of An Comhairle Ealaion (The Arts Council) in the publication of this book is gratefully acknowledged.

Poolbeg Press Ltd. acknowledge with thanks the co-operation of The Bodley Head Ltd. and Penguin Books Ltd. in the production of this collection.

Designed by Steven Hope
Cover by Robert Ballagh

Printed by Cahill Printers Limited,
East Wall Road, Dublin 3.

AUTHOR'S NOTE

I've resisted using a pin to make this selection from my Irish stories, although the temptation was strong because the task wasn't an easy one. If I'd chosen my eleven favourites the collection would have had a lopsided feel about it. If I'd chosen the ones that were superficially the most Irish, or all the ones set in a small town, or the ones about the Irish abroad, there'd equally have been something missing. So I tried to think of stories that felt right together, with not too many obsessions repeated, stories that were different and yet echoed one another – though not, I hope, too clamorously. Some — like 'Miss Smith', which might perhaps have come out of anywhere, but in fact is set in a town in Munster – are among the first stories I ever wrote. Others – 'Death in Jerusalem' and 'Attracta' – are among the most recent.

WILLIAM TREVOR

A Choice of Butchers

The upper landing of our house had brown linoleum on it
and outside each of the bedroom doors there was a small
black mat. From this square landing with its three mats and
its window overlooking the backyard there rose a flight of
uncarpeted steps that led to the attic room where Bridget,
who was our maid, slept. The stairs that descended to the
lower landing, where the bathroom and lavatory were and
where my mother and father slept, were carpeted with a
pattern of red flowers which continued downwards to a
hall that also had brown linoleum on its floor. There was a
hall-stand in the hall and beside it a high green plant in a
brass pot, and a figure of the Holy Mother on a table, all
by itself. The walls of the landing, and of the hall and the
staircase, were papered gloomily in an oatmeal shade that
had no pattern, only a pebbly roughness that was
fashionable in my childhood in our West Cork town. On
this hung two brown pictures, one of oxen dragging a
plough over rough ground at sunrise, the other of a farmer
leading a working horse towards a farmyard at the end of
the day. It was against a background of the oatmeal shade
and the oxen in the dawn that I, through the rails of the
banisters on the upper landing, saw my father kissing
Bridget at the end of one summer holiday

I had come from my room on that warm September
evening to watch for Henry Dukelow, who came up every
night to say good night to me. I had knelt down by the
banisters, with my face against them, pressing hard so that I
might be marked, so that Mr. Dukelow would laugh when
he saw me. 'God, you're tip-top,' my father said in a

whisper that travelled easily up to me, and then he put his arms around her shoulders and roughly hugged her, with his lips pressed on to her lips.

I was seven years of age, the afterthought of the family, as my father called me. My brothers and sisters were all grown up, but I didn't feel then, not yet, that my parents had given so much to them that there wasn't a lot left to give me. Once upon a time they had all been a family like any other family: the children in turn had left home, and then, when my mother should have been resting and my father finding life less demanding, I had arrived. I did not ever doubt my parents' concern for me, but for the six months that he was in our house I felt that Mr. Dukelow loved me as much as they did. 'Say good night to him for me,' I often heard my mother calling out to him as he mounted the stairs to tell me my night-time story, and I grew up thinking of my mother as a tired person because that was what she was. Her hair was going grey and her face bore a fatigued look: Mr. Dukelow said she probably didn't sleep well. There were a lot of people who didn't sleep well, he told me, sitting on my bed one night when I was seven, and I remember he went on talking about that until I must have fallen asleep myself.

Mr. Dukelow, who occupied the room next to mine, taught me to play marbles on the rough surface of our backyard. He made me an aeroplane out of heavy pieces of wood he found lying about and he explained to me that although a star could fall through the sky it would never land on the earth. He told me stories about Columbus and Vasco da Gama, and about the great emperors of Europe and the Battle of the Yellow Ford. He had a good memory for what had interested him at school, but he had forgotten as easily the rest: he had been a poor scholar, he said. He told me the plots of films he'd seen and of a play called *Paddy the Next Best Thing*. He spoke very quietly and he always answered my questions: a small man, as thin as a willow, bony and pale-faced and supposed to be delicate, different from my father. He was fifty-seven; my father fifty-nine.

In the middle of the night that my father kissed Bridget Mr. Dukelow came to my room again. He switched the light on and stood there in grey-striped pyjamas that were badly torn.

'I could hear you crying,' he said. 'What's the trouble with you?'

He wore spectacles with fine wire rims, and all his face seemed to have gone into his nose, which was thin and tapering. His greased hair was black, his hands were like a skeleton's. The first night Mr. Dukelow arrived in our house my father brought him into the kitchen, where my mother was reading the *Irish Press* at the table and Bridget was darning one of her black stockings. 'I've employed this man,' my father said, and as he stepped to one side of the doorway the bent figure of Mr. Dukelow appeared suddenly and silently, and my father gestured in the manner of a ringmaster introducing a circus act. Mr. Dukelow was carrying a cardboard suitcase that had too many clothes in it. I remember seeing the flannel material of a shirt protruding, for the case was not fastened as it was meant to be.

'What are you crying for?' he asked me on that later occasion. 'What's up with you?'

'Go away, Mr. Dukelow.'

A frown appeared on his white forehead. He went away, leaving the light on, and he returned within a minute carrying a packet of cigarettes and a cigarette-lighter I'd bought in Woolworth's in Cork and given him the Christmas before. He always smoked Craven A, claiming that they were manufactured from a superior kind of tobacco. He lit one and sat on my bed. He talked, as often he did, about the moment of his arrival at our house and how he had paused for a moment outside it.

Looking at our house from the street, you saw the brown hall door, its paintwork grained to make it seem like mahogany. There was a brass knocker and a letter-box that every morning except Sunday were cleaned with

Brasso by Bridget. To the right of the hall door, and dwarfing it, were the windows of my father's butcher shop, with its sides of mutton hanging from hooks, tripe on a white enamel dish, and beef and sausages and mince and suet.

Afterwards, when he became my friend, Mr. Dukelow said that he had stood on the street outside the shop, having just got off the Bantry bus. With his suitcase weighing him down, he had gazed at the windows, wondering about the shop and the house, and about my father. He had not come all the way from Bantry but from a house in the hills somewhere, where he had been employed as some kind of manservant. He had walked to a crossroads and had stood there waiting for the bus: there had been dust on his shoes that night when first he came into our kitchen. 'I looked at the meat in the window,' he told me afterwards, 'and I thought I'd rather go away again.' But my father, expecting him, had come out of the shop and had told him to come on in. My father was a big man; beside Mr. Dukelow he looked like a giant.

Mr. Dukelow sat on my bed, smoking his Craven A. He began to talk about the advertisement my father had placed in the *Cork Examiner* for an assistant. He repeated the words my father had employed in the advertisement and he said he'd been nervous even to look at them. 'I had no qualifications,' Mr. Dukelow said. 'I was afraid.'

That night, six months before, there'd been that kind of fear in his face. 'Sit down, Mr. Dukelow,' my mother had said. 'Have you had your tea?' He shook hands with my mother and myself and with Bridget, making a great thing of it, covering up his shyness. He said he'd had tea, although he confessed to me afterwards that he hadn't. 'You'll take a cup, anyway,' my mother offered, 'and a piece of fruit-cake I made?' Bridget took a kettle from the range and poured boiling water into a teapot to warm it. 'Errah, maybe he wants something stronger,' my father said giving a great gusty laugh. 'Will we go down to Keogh's, Henry?' But my mother insisted that, first of all, before strong drink was taken, before even Mr. Dukelow was led to his room, he should have a cup of tea and a slice of fruit-cake. 'He's hardly inside the door,' she said chidingly to my father, 'before you're lifting him out again.' My father who laughed easily, laughed again. 'Doesn't he have to get to know the people of the town?' he demanded. 'It's a great little town,' he informed Mr. Dukelow. 'There's tip-top business here.' My father had only seven fingers and one thumb: being a clumsy man, he had lost the others at different moments, when engaged in his trade. When he had no fingers left he would retire, he used to say, and he would laugh in his roaring way, and add that the sight of a butcher with no fingers would be more than customers could tolerate.

'I often think back,' said Mr. Dukelow, 'to the kindness of your mother that first time.'

'He kissed Bridget in the hall,' I said. 'He said she was looking great.'

'Ah, no.'

'I saw him through the banisters.'

'Is it a nightmare you had? Will I get your mammy up?'

I said it wasn't a nightmare I had had: I said I didn't want my mother. My mother was sleeping beside him in their bed and she'd didn't know that he'd been kissing the maid.

'She'd go away,' I said. 'My mother would go away.'

'Ah, no, no.'

'He was kissing Bridget.'

Once, saying good night to me, Mr. Dukelow had unexpectedly given me a kiss, but it was a kiss that wasn't at all like the kiss I had observed in the hall. Mr. Dukelow had kissed me because my mother was too tired to climb the stairs; he had kissed me in case I felt neglected. Another time, just as unexpectedly, he had taken a florin from his waistcoat pocket and had put it under my pillow, telling me to buy sweets with it. 'Where d'you get that from?' my father had demanded the next day, and when I told him he hit the side of his leg with his fist, becoming angry in a way that puzzled me. Afterwards I heard him shouting at my mother that Henry Dukelow had given me a two-bob bit and had she anything to say to that? My father was sometimes so peculiar in his behaviour that I couldn't make him out. My mother's quietness was always more noticeable when he was present; I loved her for her quietness.

'He had a few jars in tonight.'

'Was he drunk, Mr. Dukelow?'

'I think he was.'

'My mother—'

'Will I tell you a story?'

'No, no.'

I imagined Bridget, as I had been imagining her while I lay awake, thinking to herself that she'd give my mother her marching orders. I imagined, suddenly, my mother doing Bridget's work in the kitchen and Bridget standing at the door watching her. She was a plump girl, red-cheeked, with black curly hair. She had fat arms and legs, and she wasn't as tall as my mother. She must have been about twenty-five at the time; Mr. Dukelow had told me that my mother was fifty-one. Bridget used to bring me the green glass balls that fishermen use for floating their nets, because she lived by the sea and often found them washed up on the strand. She didn't tell me stories like Mr. Dukelow did, but sometimes she'd read to me out of one of the romances she borrowed from the library that the nuns ran. All the books had brown paper covers on them to keep them from getting dirty, with the titles written in ink on the front. I couldn't remember a time that Bridget hadn't been in the house, with those brown-covered volumes, cycling back from her Sunday afternoon off with fish and vegetables in a basket. I had always liked her, but she was different from my mother: I was fonder of my mother.

'If my mother died,' I said, 'he would be married to Bridget. She didn't mind it when he kissed her.'

Mr. Dukelow shook his head. She might have been taken unawares, he pointed out: she might have minded it and not been able to protest owing to surprise. Maybe she'd protested, he suggested, after I'd run back to bed.

'She's going out with the porter in the Munster and Leinster Bank,' he said. 'She's keen on that fellow.'

'My father's got more money.'

'Don't worry about your father now. A little thing like that can happen and that's the end of it. Your father's a decent man.'

It was typical of Mr. Dukelow to say that my father was a decent man, even though he knew my father didn't like him. In the shop Mr. Dukelow outclassed him: after he'd recovered from his initial nervousness, he'd became neater with the meat than my father was, and it was impossible to imagine Mr. Dukelow banging through his thin fingers with the cleaver, or letting a knife slip into his flesh. My father said Mr. Dukelow had a lot to learn, but it was my father really who had a lot to learn, since he hadn't been able to learn properly in the first place. Once, a women called Mrs. Tighe had returned a piece of meat to the shop, complaining that it had a smell. 'Will you watch that, Henry?' my father expostulated after Mrs. Tighe had left the shop, but Mrs. Tighe hadn't said it was Mr. Dukelow who had sold her the meat. I was there myself at the time and I knew from the expression on Mr. Dukelow's face that it was my father who had sold the bad meat to Mrs. Tighe. 'Any stuff like that,' my father said to me, 'mince up in the machine.' I could see Mr. Dukelow deciding that he intended to do no such thing: it would go against his sensitivity to mince up odorous meat, not because of the dishonesty of the action but because he had become a more prideful butcher than my father, even though he was only an assistant. Mr. Dukelow would throw such a piece of meat away, hiding it beneath offal so that my father couldn't accuse him of wasting anything.

In my bedroom, which had a yellow distemper on the walls and a chest of drawers painted white, with a cupboard and washstand to match, Mr. Dukelow told me not to worry. There was a little crucifix on the wall above my

13

bed, placed there by my mother, and there was a sacred picture opposite the bed so that I could see the face of Our Lady from where I lay. 'Say a prayer,' urged Mr. Dukelow, indicating with a thin hand the two reminders of my Faith. 'I would address St. Agnes on a question like that.'

Slowly he selected and lit another cigarette. 'Your father's a decent man,' he repeated, and then he must have gone away because when I woke up the light had been switched off. It was half past seven and the first thing I thought was that the day was the last day of the summer holidays. Then I remembered my father kissing Bridget and Mr. Dukelow talking to me in the night.

We all had our breakfast together in the kitchen, my mother at one end of the table, my father at the other, Bridget next to me, and Mr. Dukelow opposite us. We always sat like that, for all meals, but what I hadn't paid any attention to before was that Bridget was next to my father.

'Two dozen chops,' he said, sitting there with blood on his hands. 'Did I tell you that, Henry? To go over to Mrs. Ashe in the hotel.'

'I'll cut them so,' promised Mr. Dukelow in his quiet way.

My father laughed. 'Errah, man, haven't I cut them myself?' He laughed again. He watched while Bridget knelt down to open the iron door of the oven. 'There's nothing like cutting chops,' he said, 'to give you an appetite for your breakfast, Bridget.'

My eyes were on a piece of fried bread on my plate. I didn't lift them, but I could feel Mr. Dukelow looking at me. He knew I felt jealous because my father had addressed Bridget instead of my mother. I was jealous on my mother's behalf, because she couldn't be jealous herself, because she didn't know. Mr. Dukelow sensed everything, as though there was an extra dimension to him. The chops for Mrs. Ashe would have been more elegantly cut if he had cut them himself; they'd have been more cleverly cut, with less waste and in half the time.

'Ah, that's great,' said my father as Bridget placed a plate of rashers and sausages in front of him. She sat down quietly beside me. Neither she nor my mother had said anything since I'd entered the kitchen.

'Is there no potato cakes?' my father demanded, and my mother said she'd be making fresh ones today.

'The last ones were lumpy.'

'A little,' agreed my mother. 'There were a few little lumps.'

He held his knife and fork awkwardly because of the injuries to his hands. Often he put too much on his fork and pieces of bacon would fall off. Mr. Dukelow, when he was eating, had a certain style.

'Well, mister-me-buck,' said my father, addressing me, 'it's the final day of your holidays.'

'Yes.'

'When I was the age you are I had to work in my holidays. I was delivering meat at six and a half years.'

'Yes.'

'Don't the times change, Bridget?'

Bridget said that times did change. My father asked Mr. Dukelow if he had worked during the holidays as a child and Mr. Dukelow replied that he had worked in the fields in the summertime, weeding, harvesting potatoes, and making hay.

'They have an easy time of it these days,' my father pronounced. He had addressed all of us except my mother. He pushed his cup towards Bridget and she passed it to my mother for more tea.

'An easy time of it,' repeated my father.

I could see him eyeing Mr. Dukelow's hands as if he was thinking to himself that they didn't look as if they would be much use for harvesting potatoes. And I thought to myself that my father was wrong in this estimation: Mr. Dukelow would collect the potatoes speedily, having dug them himself in a methodical way; he would toss them into sacks with a flick of the wrist, a craftsman even in that.

The postman, called Mr. Dicey, who was small and inquisitive and had squinting eyes, came into the kitchen from the yard. When he had a letter for the household he delivered it in this manner, while we sat at breakfast. He would stand while the letter was opened, drinking a cup of tea.

'That's a fine morning,' said Mr. Dicey. 'We'll have a fine day of it.'

'Unless it rains.' My father laughed until he was red in the face, and then abruptly ceased because no one was laughing with him. 'How're you, Dicey?' he more calmly inquired.

'I have an ache in my back,' replied Mr. Dicey, handing my mother a letter.

Mr. Dukelow nodded at him, greeting him in that way. Sometimes Mr. Dukelow was so quiet in the kitchen that my father asked him if there was something awry with him.

'I was saying to the bucko here,' said my father, 'that when I was his age I used to deliver meat from the shop. Haven't times changed, Dicey?'

'They have not remained the same,' agreed Mr. Dicey. 'You could not expect it.'

Bridget handed him a cup of tea. He stirred sugar into it, remarking to Bridget that he'd seen her out last night. It was said that Mr. Dicey's curiosity was so great he often steamed open a letter and delivered it a day late. He was interested in everyone in the town and was keen to know of fresh developments in people's lives.

'You didn't see me at all,' he said to Bridget. He paused, drinking his tea. 'You were engaged at the same time,' he said, 'with another person.'

'Oh, Bridie has her admirers all right,' said my father.

'From the Munster and Leinster Bank.' Mr. Dicey laughed. 'There's a letter from your daughter,' he said to my mother. 'I know her little round-shaped writing.'

My mother, concerned with the letter, nodded.

'Bridie could claim the best,' said my father.

I looked at him and saw that he was glancing down the length of the table at my mother.

'Bridie could claim the best,' he repeated in a notably loud voice. 'Wouldn't you say that, Dicey? Isn't she a great-looking girl?'

'She is, of course,' said Mr. Dicey. 'Why shouldn't she be?'

'It's a wonder she never claimed Henry Dukelow.' My father coughed and laughed. 'Amn't I right she could claim the best, Henry? Couldn't Bridie have any husband she put her eye on?'

'I'll carry over the chops to Mrs. Ashe,' said Mr. Dukelow, getting up from the table.

My father laughed. 'Henry Dukelow wouldn't be interested,' he said. 'D'you understand me, Dicey?'

'Oh, now, why wouldn't Henry be interested?' inquired Mr. Dicey, interested himself.

Mr. Dukelow washed his hands at the sink. He dried them on a towel that hung on the back of the kitchen door, a special towel that only he and my father used.

'He's not a marrying man,' said my father. 'Amn't I right, Henry?'

Mr. Dukelow smiled at my father and left the kitchen without speaking. Mr. Dicey began to say something, but my father interrupted him.

'He's not a marrying man,' he repeated. He pressed a piece of bread into the grease on his plate. He cleaned the plate with it, and then ate it and drank some tea. Mr. Dicey put his cup and saucer on the table, telling Bridget she was a marvel at making tea. There wasn't better tea in the town, Mr. Dicey said, than the tea he drank in this kitchen. He wanted to remain, to hang around in case something happened: he was aware of a heavy atmosphere that morning and he was as puzzled as I was.

My mother was still reading the letter, my father was still staring at her head. Was he trying to hurt her? I wondered: was he attempting to upset her by saying that Bridget could have anyone she wanted as a husband?

17

She handed the letter to me, indicating that I should pass it on to him. I saw that it was from my sister Sheila, who had married, two Christmases before, a salesman of stationery. I gave it to my father and I watched him reading.

'Bedad,' he said. 'She's due for a baby.'

When I heard my father saying that I thought for only a moment about what the words signified. Bridget exclaimed appropriately, and then there was a silence while my father looked at my mother. She smiled at him in a half-hearted way, obliged by duty to do that, reluctant to share any greater emotion with him.

'Is it Sheila herself?' cried Mr. Dicey in simulated excitement. 'God, you wouldn't believe it!' From the way he spoke it was evident that he had known the details of the letter. He went on to say that it seemed only yesterday that my sister was an infant herself. He continued to talk, his squinting eyes moving rapidly over all of us, and I could sense his interest in the calm way my mother had taken the news, not saying a word. There was a damper on the natural excitement, which no one could have failed to be aware of.

My father tried to make up for the lack of commotion by shouting out that for the first time in his life he would be a grandfather. My mother smiled again at him and then, like Mr. Dukelow, she rose and left the kitchen. Reluctantly, Mr. Dicey took his leave of us also.

Bridget collected the dishes from the table and conveyed them to the sink. My father lit a cigarette. He poured himself a cup of tea, humming a melody that often, tunelessdy, he did hum. 'You're as quiet as Henry Dukelow this morning,' he said to me, and I wanted to reply that we were all quiet except himself, but I didn't say anything. Sometimes when he looked at me I rememebered the time he'd said to me that he wondered when I was grown up if I'd take over his shop and be a butcher like he was. 'Your brothers didn't care for that,' he said, speaking without rancour but with a certain sorrow in his voice. 'They didn't fancy the trade.' He had smiled at me coaxingly, saying that he was a happy man and that he had built up the business and wouldn't want to see it die away. At the time I felt revulsion at the thought of cutting up dead animals all day long, knifing off slices of red steak and poking for kidneys. I had often watched him at work since he encouraged me to do that, even offering me the experience as a treat. 'Well, mister-me-buck,' he would shout at me, bustling about in his white apron, 'is there a nice piece of liver there for Mrs. Bourke?' He would talk to his customers about me as he weighed their orders, remarking that I was growing well and was a good boy when I remembered to be. 'Will you be a butcher like your daddy?' a woman often asked me and I could feel the tension in him without at the time understanding it. It wasn't until I saw Mr. Dukelow going about the business in his stylish way that I began to say to the women that I might be a butcher one day. Mr. Dukelow didn't make me feel that he was cutting up dead animals at all: Mr. Dukelow made it all seem civilised.

I didn't leave the kitchen that morning until my father had finished his cup of tea and was ready to go also, in case he'd kiss Bridget when they were alone together. He told me to hurry up and go and help my mother, but I delayed deliberately and in the end I shamed him into going before me. Bridget went on cleaning the dishes in the sink, standing there silently, as if she didn't know what was happening.

I went to my parents' bedroom, where my mother was making their bed. She asked me to take the end of a sheet and to pull it up so that she wouldn't have to walk around the bed and do it herself. She had taught me how to help her. I seized the end of the sheet and then the end of a blanket. I said:

'If you go away I will go with you.'

She looked at me. She asked me what I'd said and I said it again. She didn't reply. We went on making the bed together and when it was finished, she said:

'It isn't me who's going away, love.'

'Is it Bridget?'

'There's no need for Bridget —'

'I saw him —'

'He didn't mean any harm.'

'Did you see him too?'

'It doesn't matter at all. Sheila's going to have a little baby. Isn't that grand?'

I couldn't understand why she was suddenly talking about my sister having a baby since it had nothing to do with my father kissing Bridget.

'It's not he who's going away?' I asked, knowing that for my father to go away would be the most unlikely development of all.

'Bridget was telling me yesterday,' my mother said, 'she's going to marry the porter at the Munster and Leinster Bank. It's a secret Bridget has: don't tell your father or Mr. Dicey or anyone like that.'

'Mr. Dukelow —'

'It is Mr. Dukelow who will be going away.'

She covered the big bed with a candlewick bedspread. She pointed a finger at the side of the bedspread that was near me, indicating that I should aid her with it.

'Mr. Dukelow?' I said. 'Why would —'

'He moves around from one place to another. He does different kinds of work.'

'Does he get the sack?'

My mother shrugged her shoulders. I went on asking questions, but she told me to be quiet. I followed her to the kitchen and watched her making potato cakes, while Bridget went in and out. Occasionally they spoke, but they weren't unfriendly: it wasn't between them that there was anything wrong. I remembered Bridget saying to me one time that my mother was always very good to her, better than her own mother had even been. She had a great fondness for my mother, she said, and I sensed it between them that morning because somehow it seemed greater than it had been in the past, even though the night before my father had been kissing Bridget in the hall. I kept looking at my mother, wanting her to explain whatever there was to explain to me, to tell me why Mr. Dukelow, who'd said he never wanted to leave my father's shop, was going to leave now, after only six months. I couldn't imagine the house without Mr. Dukelow. I couldn't imagine lying in my bed without anyone to come and tell me about Vasco da Gama. I couldn't imagine not seeing him lighting a Craven A cigarette from the little lighter I'd bought him.

'Well, isn't that terrible?' said my father when we were all sitting down again at the kitchen table for our dinner. 'Henry Dukelow's shifting on.'

Mr. Dukelow looked nervous. He glanced from me to my mother, not knowing that my mother had guessed he would be going, not knowing she'd suggested it to me.

'We thought he might be,' my mother said. 'He's learnt the business.'

My father pressed potatoes into his mouth and remarked on the stew we were eating. His mood was wholly different now: he wagged his head at my mother, saying she'd cooked the meat well. There wasn't a woman in the country, he tediously continued, who could cook stew like my mother. He asked me if I agreed with that, and I said I did. 'You'll be back at school tomorrow,' he said, and I agreed with that also. 'Tell them they'll have an uncle in the class,' he advised, 'and give the teacher a few smiles.'

Releasing an obstreperous laugh, he pushed his plate away from him with the stumps of two fingers. 'Will we go down to Keogh's,' he suggested to Mr. Dukelow, 'and have a talk about what you will do?'

'You can talk here,' said my mother with severity. I could see her saying to herself that it was the half-day and if my father entered Keogh's he'd remain there for the afternoon.

'Hurry up, Henry,' said my father, scraping his chair as he pushed it back on the flagged floor. 'A tip-top stew,' he repeated. He made a noise in his mouth, sucking through his teeth, a noise that was familiar to all of us. He told Mr.

Dukelow he'd be waiting for him in Keogh's.

'Keep an eye on him,' my mother murmured when he'd gone, and Mr. Dukelow nodded.

'I would have told you that tonight,' he said to me. 'I didn't want to say a thing until I'd mentioned it to your father first.'

'Mr. Dukelow'll be here a month yet.' My mother smiled at me. 'He can tell you a good few stories in that time.'

But Mr. Dukelow in fact did not remain in our house for another month. When he returned with my father later that day, my father, in a better mood than ever, said:

'We've come to a good agreement. Henry's going to pack his traps. He'll catch the half seven bus.'

But Mr. Dukelow didn't say anything. He walked from the kitchen without swaying like my father was swaying.

My father had his hat on and he didn't take it off. He took his turnip watch from his waistcoat pocket and examined it. 'I can't see without my glasses,' he said to me. 'Will you take a gander at it, boy?'

He never wore glasses, but he often made the joke when he'd been down to Keogh's for a while. I told him it was twenty past six. He put the stumps of two fingers on my head and said I was a great boy. Did I know, he asked me, that in six months' time I'd be an uncle? He had a way of touching me with his stumps instead of with the fingers that remained with him, just as he had a way of pushing from him a plate from which he'd eaten a meal. 'Don't forget to tell the teacher,' he said. 'It's not every day he has an uncle to instruct.'

My mother took a barm brack from a tin and began to butter it for Mr. Dukelow before he went. Bridget moved a kettle on to the hot areas of the stove. It boiled at once. 'Will I fry him something?' she asked my mother.

'There's rashers there,' said my mother, 'and a bit of black pudding. Do him eggs, Bridget, and a few potato cakes.'

'He's going,' repeated my father. His face, redder than

usually it was, had sweat on the sides of it. 'He's going,' he said again.

I was sitting at the end of the table with a comic spread out in front of me. While I gazed at my father half my vision retained the confused mass of cartoon characters.

'Well, that's that,' said my father.

He stood there swaying, his feet rooted to the kitchen floor, like a statue about to topple in a wind. He was wearing the blue-striped suit that he always wore on the half-day; his hands were hanging by his sides.

'You should be bloody ashamed of yourself,' he said suddenly, and I thought he was talking to me. He wasn't looking at any of us; his eyes were turned upwards, regarding a corner of the ceiling. 'A chancer like that,' he said, 'that gives a young fellow two-bob pieces.' Instinctively I knew then that he was speaking to my mother, even though she did not acknowledge his remarks.

'Sent up from Satan,' he said. 'Sent up to make wickedness. I'm sorry about that thing, Bridget.'

Bridget shook her head, implying that it didn't matter, and I knew they were referring to what had happened in the hall last night.

'Tell Henry Dukelow I'll see him at the bus.' He moved to the back door, adding that he was returning to Keogh's until it was time to say good-bye to Mr. Dukelow. 'He'll never make a butcher,' he said, 'or any other bloody thing either.'

I closed the comic and watched my mother and Bridget preparing Mr. Dukelow's last meal in our house. They didn't speak and I was afraid to, now. I still couldn't understand why this series of events was taking place. I tried to connect one occurrence with another, but I failed. I felt forgotten in the house: I might have been dead at the table for all they considered me: they were assuming I had no mind.

Mr. Dukelow came into the silence, carrying the suitcase he had first carried into the kitchen six months ago, bound up with what looked like the same piece of string. He ate in silence, and Bridget and my mother sat at the table, not saying anything either. I pretended to read the comic, but all the time I was thinking that I'd rather have Mr. Dukelow for my father. I couldn't help thinking it and I began to imagine my father sitting on the Bantry bus and Mr. Dukelow staying where he was, running the shop better than my father had ever run it, cutting the meat better. I thought of Mr. Dukelow in the big bed with my mother, lying asleep beside her. I saw his hands on the white sheets, the thin clever hands instead of hands that made you turn your head away. I saw Mr. Dukelow and my mother and myself going out for a walk together on a Sunday afternoon, and Mr. Dukelow telling us about Vasco da Gama and Columbus. Mr. Dukelow could spend the afternoon in Keogh's and not sway and lurch when he came back. There was no need for Mr. Dukelow to go kissing the maid.

'I'm sorry I upset him,' said Mr. Dukelow suddenly. 'He's a decent man.'

'It has nothing to do with anything,' said my mother. 'He's in a bad way with drink.'

'Yes,' said Mr. Dukelow.

As out of a fog the truth came in pieces to me, and some of the pieces as yet were missing. In six months Mr. Dukelow had become a better butcher than my father and my father was jealous of that. Jealousy had caused him to see Mr. Dukelow as a monster; jealousy had spread from him in different directions until it wrapped my mother and myself, and tortured my father's pride until he felt he must get his own back and prove himself in some way.

'I'll say good-bye,' said Mr. Dukelow, and I hated my father then for his silly pettiness. I wanted Mr. Dukelow to go to my mother and kiss her as my father had kissed Bridget. I wanted him to kiss Bridget too, in a way more elegant than the way of my father.

But none of that happened, nor did I ask why, in the face of everything, my father was being described as a decent man. Mr. Dukelow left the kitchen, having shaken hands with the three of us. I sat down again at the table while my mother and Bridget prepared the tea. They did not say anything, but I thought to myself that I could see in Bridget's flushed face a reflection of what was passing in her mind: that Mr. Dukelow was a nicer man than the porter at the Munster and Leinster Bank. My mother's face was expressionless, but I thought to myself that I knew what expression would be there if my mother cared to permit its presence.

Again I pretended I was reading the comic, but all the time I was thinking about what had silently occurred in our house and how for no sensible reason at all my father's rumbustiousness had spoilt everything. No one but my father could not love Mr. Dukelow: no one in the wide world, I thought, except that red-faced man with stumps on his hands, who fell over chairs when he'd been down in Keogh's, who swayed and couldn't read the time. I thought about the ugliness of my father's jealous nature and the gentleness it had taken exception to. 'Sent up from Satan,' his stumbling voice had ridiculously announced. 'Sent up to make wickedness.' How could it be, I wondered, that I was the child of one instead of the other?

'Well, mister-me-buck,' said my father, returning to the kitchen after a time. When I looked at him I began to cry and my mother took me up to bed, saying I was tired.

Memories of Youghal

He did not, he said, remember the occasion of his parents'
death, having been at the time only five months old. His
first memory was of a black iron gate, of his own hand
upon a part of it, and of his uncle driving through the
gateway in a model-T Ford. These images, and that of his
uncle's bespectacled face perspiring, were all in sunshine.
For him, so he said to Miss Ticher, the sunlight still glim-
mered on the dim black paint of the motor-car; his uncle,
cross and uncomfortable on hot upholstery, did not smile.

He remembered also, at some later time, eating tinned
tomato soup in a house that was not the house of his aunt
and uncle; he remembered a tap near a greenhouse; he
remembered eating an ice-cream outside Horgan's Picture
House while his aunt engaged another woman in conversation. Pierrots performed on the sands; a man who seemed
to be a priest gave him a Fox's Glacier Mint.

'The gate was tarred, I think,' he said. 'A tarred black
gate. That memory is the first of all.'

The elderly woman to whom he spoke smiled at him,
covering with the smile the surprise she experienced
because a stout, untidy stranger spoke to her so easily about
his memories.

'I recall my uncle eating the tinned tomato soup,' the
man said, 'and my aunt, who was a severe woman, giving
him a disapproving glance because of the row he was kick-
ing up with it. The tap near the greenhouse came from a
pipe that rose crookedly out of the ground.'

'I see,' she said, smiling a little more. She added that her
own earliest memory, as far as she could remember, was of

a papier-mache spotted dog filled with sweets. The man didn't comment on that.

'Horgan's Picture House,' he said. 'I wonder is it still going strong?'

She shook her head. She said she didn't know if Horgan's Picture House was still standing, since she had never been to the town he spoke of.

'I first saw Gracie Fields there,' he revealed. 'And Jack Hulbert in a funny called *Round the Washtub*.'

They were reclining in deck-chairs on a terrace of the Hotel Les Galets in Bandol, looking out at the Mediterranean. Mimosa and bougainvillaea bloomed around them, oranges ripened, palm trees flapped in a small breeze, and on a pale-blue sky the sun pushed hazy clouds aside. With her friend Miss Grimshaw, Miss Ticher always came to Bandol in late April, between the mistral and the season, before the noise and the throbbing summer heat. They had known one another for more than thirty years and when, next year, they both retired at sixty-five they planned to live in a bungalow in Sevenoaks, not far from St. Mildred's School for Girls, where Miss Ticher taught history and Miss Grimshaw French. They would, they hoped, continue to travel in the spring to Bandol, to the quiet Mediterranean and *soupe de poissons*, their favourite dish.

Miss Ticher was a thin woman with a shy face and frail, thin hands. She had been asleep on the upper terrace of Les Galets and had wakened to find the untidy man standing in front of her. He had asked if he might sit in the deck-chair beside hers, the chair that Miss Grimshaw had earlier planned to occupy on her return from her walk. Miss Ticher felt she could not prevent the man from sitting down, and so had nodded. He was not staying in the hotel, he said, and added that his business was that of a detective. He was observing a couple who were at present in an upstairs room: it would facilitate his work if Miss Ticher would kindly permit him to remain with her and perhaps engage in a casual conversation while he awaited the couple's emergence. A detective, he told Miss Ticher, could not be obvious: a detective must blend with the background, or at least seem natural. 'The So-Swift Investigation Agency', he said. 'A London firm.' As he lowered himself into the chair that Miss Grimshaw had reserved for herself he said he was an exiled Irishman. 'Did you ever hear of the Wild Geese?' he enquired. 'Soldiers of fortune? I often feel like that myself. My name is Roche.'

He was younger than he looked, she thought: forty-five, she estimated, and seeming to be ten years older. Perhaps it was that, looking older than he was, or perhaps it was the uneasy emptiness in his eyes that made her feel sorry for him. His eyes apologised for himself, even though he attempted to hide the apology beneath a jauntiness. He wouldn't be long on the terrace, he promised: the couple would soon be checking out of the hotel and on behalf of the husband of the woman he would discreetly follow them, around the coast in a hired Renault. It was work he did not much care for, but it was better than other work he had experienced: he'd drifted about, he added with a laugh, from pillar to post. With his eyes closed in the warmth he talked about his childhood memories while Miss Ticher listened.

'Youghal,' he said. 'I was born in Youghal, in Co. Cork. In 1934 my mother went in for a swim and got caught up with a current. My dad went out to fetch her and they both went down.'

He left his deck-chair and went away, and strangely she wondered if perhaps he was going to find a place to weep. An impression of his face remained with her: a fat red face with broken veins in it, and blue eyes beneath dark brows. When he smiled he revealed teeth that were stained and chipped and not his own. Once, when laughing over a childhood memory, they had slipped from their position in his jaw and had had to be replaced. Miss Ticher had looked away in embarrassment, but he hadn't minded at all. He wasn't a man who cared about the way he struck other people. His trousers were held up with a tie, his pale stomach showed through an unbuttoned shirt. There was dandruff in his sparse fluff of sandy hair and on the shoulders of a blue blazer: yesterday's dandruff, Miss Ticher had thought, or even the day before's.

'I've brought you this,' he said, returning and sitting again in the Miss Grimshaw's chair. He proffered a glass of red liquid. 'A local aperitif.'

Over pots of geraniums and orange-tiled roofs, across the bay and the green sea that was ruffled with little bursts of foam, were the white villas of Sanary, set among cypresses. Nearer, and more directly below, was the road to Toulon and beyond it a scrappy beach on which Miss Ticher now observed the figure of Miss Grimshaw.

'I was given over to the aunt and uncle,' said Roche, 'on the day of the tragedy. Although, as I'm saying to you, I don't remember it.'

He drank whisky mixed with ice. He shook the liquid in his glass, watching it. He offered Miss Ticher a cigarette, which she refused. He lit one himself.

'The uncle kept a shop,' he said.

She saw Miss Grimshaw crossing the road to Toulon. A driver hooted; Miss Grimshaw took no notice.

'Memories are extraordinary,' said Roche, 'the things you'd remember and the things you wouldn't. I went to the infant class at the Loreto Convent. There was a Sister Tracy. I remember a woman with a red face who cried one time. There was a boy called Joe Murphy whose grandmother kept a greengrocer's. I was a member of Joe Murphy's gang. We used to fight another gang.'

Miss Grimshaw passed from view. She would be approaching the hotel, moving slowly in the warmth, her sun-burnt face shining as her spectacles shone. She would arrive panting, and already, in her mind, Miss Ticher could hear her voice. 'What on earth's that red stuff you're drinking?' she'd demand in a huffy manner.

'When I was thirteen years old I ran away from the aunt and uncle,' Roche said. 'I hooked up with a travelling entertainments crowd that used to go about the seaside places. I think the aunt must have been the happy female that day. She couldn't stand the sight of me.'

'Oh surely now —'

'Listen,' said Roche, leaning closer to Miss Ticher and staring intently into her eyes. 'I'll tell you the way this case was: are you interested?'

'Well —'

'The uncle had no interest of any kind in the bringing up of a child. The uncle's main interest was drinking bottles of stout in Phelan's public house, with Macnamara the butcher. The aunt was a different kettle of fish: the aunt above all things wanted nippers of her own. For the whole of my thirteen years in that house I was a reminder to my aunt of her childless condition. I was a damn nuisance to both of them.'

Miss Ticher, moved by these revelations, did not know what to say. His eyes were slightly bloodshot, she saw; and then she thought it was decidedly an odd thing, a detective going on about his past to an elderly woman on the terrace of an hotel.

'I wasn't wanted in that house,' he said. 'When I was five years old she told me the cost of the food I ate.'

It would have been 1939 when he was five, she thought, and she remembered herself in 1939, a girl of twenty-four, just starting her career at St. Mildred's, a girl who'd begun to feel that marriage, which she'd wished for, might not come her way. 'We're neither of us the type,' Miss Grimshaw later said. 'We'd be lost, my dear, without the busy life of school.'

She didn't want Miss Grimshaw to arrive on the terrace. She wanted this man who was a stranger to her to go on talking in his sentimental way. He described the town he spoke of: an ancient gateway and a main street, and a harbour where fishing boats went from, and the strand with wooden breakwaters where his parents had drowned, and seaside boarding-houses and a promenade, and short grass on a clay hill above the sea.

'Near the lighthouse in Youghal,' said Roche, 'there's a

shop I used to buy Rainbow Toffees in.'

Miss Grimshaw appeared on the terrace and walked towards them. She was a small plump woman with grey hair, and short legs and short arms. Generations of girls at St. Mildred's had likened her to a ball and had, among themselves, named her appropriately. She wore now a flowered dress and carried in her left hand a yellow plastic bag containing the fruits of her morning's excursion: a number of shells.

'At a later time,' said Roche, 'I joined the RAF in order to get a polish. I knocked about the world a bit, making do the best way I could. And then a few years back I entered the investigation business.'

Miss Grimshaw, annoyed because an unprepossessing man in a blazer was sprawling in her chair, saw that her friend was holding in her hand a glass of red liquid and was further annoyed because of this: they pooled their resources at the beginning of each holiday and always consulted each other before making a purchase. Ignoring the sprawling man, she asked Miss Ticher what the glass contained, speaking sharply to register her disapproval and disappointment. She stood, since there was no chair for her to sit on.

'I never went back to Youghal,' the man said before Miss Ticher could reply to Miss Grimshaw's query. 'I only have the childhood memories of it now. Unhappy memories,' said the man to Miss Grimshaw's amazement. 'Unhappy memories of a nice little place. That's life for you.'

'It's an aperitif,' said Miss Ticher, 'that Mr. Roche kindly bought for me. Mr. Roche, this is Miss Grimshaw, my friend.'

'We were discussing memories,' said Roche, pushing himself out of the deck-chair. 'Miss Ticher and myself were going down Memory Lane.' He laughed loudly, causing the teeth to move about in his mouth. His shoes were scuffed, Miss Grimshaw noted; the blue scarf that was stuck into the open neck of his shirt seemed dirty.

Again he walked abruptly away. He offered Miss Grimshaw no greeting and Miss Ticher no farewell. He moved along the terrace with the glass in his hand and a cigarette in his mouth. His trousers bagged at the back, requiring to be hitched up.

'Who on earth's that?' demanded Miss Grimshaw. 'You never let him pay for that stuff you're drinking?'

'He's a detective,' said Miss Ticher. 'He's watching a couple for a husband. He followed them here.'

'Followed?'

'He's in the investigation business nowadays.'

Miss Grimshaw sat in the chair the man had been sitting in. Her eyes returned to the glass of red intoxicant her friend was still holding. She thought to herself that she had gone out alone, looking for shells because Agnes Ticher had said she was tired that morning, and the next thing was Agnes Ticher had got herself involved with a bore.

'He smelt,' said Miss Grimshaw. 'I caught a most unwelcome little whiff.'

'His whisky,' Miss Ticher began. 'Whisky has a smell —'

'You know what I mean, Agnes,' said Miss Grimshaw quietly.

'Did you enjoy your walk?'

Miss Grimshaw nodded. She said it was a pity that Miss Ticher hadn't accompanied her. She felt much better after the exercise. She had an appetite for lunch after the salt of the sea in her nostrils. She looked again at the glass in Miss Ticher's hand, implying with her glance that the consumption of refreshment before lunch could serve only to fatigue whatever appetite Miss Ticher had managed to gain in the course of her idle morning.

'My God,' said Miss Grimshaw, 'he's coming back.'

He was coming towards them with another deck-chair. Behind him walked a waiter bearing on a tin tray three glasses, two containing the red liquid that Miss Ticher was drinking, the third containing ice and whisky. Without speaking, he set up the deck-chair, facing both of them.

The waiter moved an ornamental table and placed the glasses on it.

'A local aperitif,' said Roche. 'I wouldn't touch it myself, Miss Grimshaw.'

He laughed and again had difficulty with his teeth. Miss Ticher looked away when his fingers rose to his mouth to settle them back into place, but Miss Grimshaw was unable to take her eyes off him. False teeth were common enough today, she was thinking: there was no need at all for them to come leaping from the jaw like that. Somehow it seemed typical of this man that he wouldn't bother to have them attended to.

'Miss Ticher and Miss Grimshaw,' said Roche slowly, as though savouring the two names. He drank some whisky. 'Miss Ticher and Miss Grimshaw,' he said again. 'You're neither of you a married woman. I didn't marry myself. I was put off marriage, to tell you the truth, by the aunt and uncle down in Youghal. It was an unnatural association, as I saw from an early age. And then of course the investigation business doesn't exactly encourage a fellow to tie up his loose ends with a female. My mother swam into the sea,' he said, addressing Miss Grimshaw and seeming to be pleased to have an opportunity to retail the story again. 'My dad swam in to get her back. They went down to the bottom like a couple of pennies. I was five months old.'

'How horrible,' said Miss Grimshaw.

'If it hadn't happened I'd be a different type of man to-day. Would you believe that? Would you agree with me, Miss Grimshaw?'

'What?'

'Would I be a different type of man if the parents had lived? When I was thirteen years of age I ran away with an entertainments crowd. I couldn't stand the house a minute more. My uncle never said a word to me, the aunt used look away when she saw me coming. Meals were taken in silence.' He paused, seeming to consider all that. Then he said: 'Youghal's a place like this place, Miss Grimshaw, stuck out on the sea. You know what I mean?'

Miss Grimshaw said she did know what he meant. He talked a lot, she thought, and in a most peculiar way. Agnes Ticher was keeping herself quiet, which no doubt was due to her embarrassment at having involved them both with such a character.

'I have another memory,' said Roche, 'that I can't place at all. It is a memory of a woman's face and often it keeps coming and going in my mind when I'm trying to sleep in bed. Like the black iron gate, it's always been there, a vague type of face that I can discern and yet I can't. D'you know what I mean?'

'Yes,' said Miss Ticher.

Miss Grimshaw shook her head.

'I told a nun about it one time, when I was a little lad, and she said it was maybe my mother. But I don't believe that for an instant. Will I tell you what I think about that face?'

Miss Ticher smiled, and seeing the smile and noting as well a flush on her friend's cheeks, it occurred to Miss Grimshaw that Agnes Ticher, having been imbibing a drink that might well have been more intoxicating than it seemed, was by now a little tipsy. There was an expression in Agnes Ticher's eyes that suggested such a condition to Miss Grimshaw; there was a looseness about her lips. In a playful way, she thought, she would tell the story in the common-room when they returned to St. Mildred's: how Agnes Ticher had been picked up by a ne'er-do-well Irishman and had ended up in a squiffy condition. Miss Grimshaw wanted to laugh, but prevented herself.

'What I think is this,' said Roche. 'The face is the face of a woman who tried to steal me out of my pram one day when the aunt left the pram outside Pasley's grocer's shop. A childless woman heard about the tragedy and said to herself that she'd take the child and be a mother to it.'

'Did a woman do that?' cried Miss Ticher, and Miss Grimshaw looked at her in amusement.

'They'd never bother to tell me,' said Roche. 'I have only the instinct to go on. Hi,' he shouted to the waiter who was hovering at the distant end of the terrace. 'Encore, encore. Trois verres, s'il vous plait.'

'Oh no,' murmured Miss Ticher.

Miss Grimshaw laughed.

'An unmarried woman like yourselves,' said Roche, 'who wanted a child. I would be a different man today if she had succeeded in doing what she wanted to do. She would have taken me away to another town, maybe to Cork, or up to Dublin. I would have different memories now. D'you understand me, Miss Grimshaw?'

The waiter came with the drinks. He took away the used glasses.

'If I close my eyes,' said Roche, 'I can see the whole episode: the woman bent over the pram and her hands going out to the orphan child. And then the aunt comes out of Pasley's and asks her what she thinks she's doing. I remember one time the aunt beating me on the legs with a bramble stick. I used eat things from the kitchen cupboard. I used bite into Chivers' jellies, I well remember that.' he paused. He said: 'If ever you're down that way, go into Youghal. It's a great place for fresh fish.'

Miss Grimshaw heard voices and looked past Miss Ticher and saw a man and a woman leaving the hotel. They stood for a moment beside the waiter at the far end of the terrace. The woman laughed. The waiter went away.

'That's the pair,' said Roche. 'They're checking out.'

He tilted his glass, draining a quantity of whisky into his mouth.

The man, wearing dark glasses and dressed in red trousers and a black leather jacket, lit his companion's cigarette. His arm was on the woman's shoulder. The waiter brought them each a drink.

'Are they looking this way, Miss Grimshaw?'

He crouched in the deck-chair, anxious not to be observed. Miss Grimshaw said the man and the woman seemed to be absorbed in one another.

'A right couple to be following around,' Roche said

with sarcasm and a hint of bitterness. 'A right vicious couple.'

Suddenly and to Miss Grimshaw's discomfiture, Miss Ticher stretched out an arm and touched with the tips of her fingers the back of the detective's large hand. 'I'm sorry,' Miss Ticher said quietly. 'I'm sorry your parents were drowned. I'm sorry you don't like the work you do.'

He shrugged away the sympathy, although he seemed not surprised to have received it. He said again that if his parents had not drowned he would not be the man they saw in front of them. He was obsessed by that idea, Miss Grimshaw considered. If the woman had succeeded in taking him from the pram he would not be the man he was either, he said: he'd had no luck in his childhood. 'It's a nice little seaside resort and yet I can never think of it without a shiver because of the bad luck that was there for me. When I think of the black iron gate and the uncle sweating in the Ford car I think of everything else as well. The woman wanted a child, Miss Ticher. A child needs love.'

'A woman too,' whispered Miss Ticher.

'But the woman's a figment of Mr. Roche's imagination,' Miss Grimshaw said with a laugh. 'He made up the story to suit some face in his mind. Couldn't it be, Mr. Roche, that the woman's face was the face of any woman at all?'

'Ah, of course, of course,' agreed Roche, glancing surreptitiously at the couple he was employed to glance at. 'You can never know certainly about a business like that.'

The couple, having finished their two drinks, descended a flight of stone steps that led from the terrace to the terrace below, and then went on down to the courtyard of the hotel. The waiter followed them, carrying their luggage. Roche stood up.

Miss Ticher imagined ironing his blazer. She imagined his face as a child. For a moment, affected as she afterwards thought by the red aperitif, it seemed that Miss Grimshaw was the stranger: Miss Grimshaw was a round woman, unknown to either of them, who had materialised suddenly, looking for a chat. Having no one's blazer to iron herself, Miss Grimshaw was jealous, for in her life she had known only friendship.

'In 1934,' said Miss Ticher, 'when you were five months old, Mr. Roche, I was still hopeful of marriage. A few years later I would have understood the woman who wished to take you from your pram.'

Miss Ticher's face was crimson as she spoke those words. She saw Miss Grimshaw looking at it. She saw her looking at her as she clambered to her feet and held a hand out to the detective. 'Goodbye,' Miss Ticher said. 'It was nice to hear your childhood memories.'

He went away in his abrupt manner. They watched him walking the length of the terrace. Miss Ticher watched his descent to the courtyard.

'My dear,' said Miss Grimshaw with her laugh, 'he bowled you over.' The story for the common-room was even better now. 'A fat man,' Miss Grimshaw heard herself saying on the first evening of term, 'who talked to Agnes about his childhood memories in a place called Youghal. He had fantasies as well, about some woman pilfering him from his pram, as though a woman would. In her tipsiness Agnes entered into all of it. I thought she'd cry.'

Miss Ticher sat down and sipped the drink the man had bought her. Miss Grimshaw said:

'Thank heavens he's not staying here.'

'You shouldn't have said he made up that story.'

'Why ever not?'

'You hurt him.'

'Hurt him?' cried Miss Grimshaw.

'He's the victim of his wretched childhood —'

'You're tipsy, Agnes.'

Miss Ticher drank the last of her red aperitif, and Miss Grimshaw glared through her shining spectacles, thinking that her friend looked as if she'd just put down a cheap romantic novel.

'It's time for lunch,' announced Miss Grimshaw snappishly, rising to her feet. 'Come on now.'

Miss Ticher shook her head. 'Near the lighthouse there's a shop,' she said, 'that sold in those days Rainbow Toffees. A woman like you or me might have seen there a child who ran away from loneliness.'

'Lunch, dear,' said Miss Grimshaw.

'How very cruel the world is.'

Miss Grimshaw, who in reply had been about to say with asperity that no one must let emotional nonsense play tricks on the imagination, instead said nothing at all. Three unnamed drinks and the conversation of a grubby detective had taken an absurd toll of Agnes Ticher in the broad light of day. Miss Grimshaw no longer wished to think about the matter; she did not wish to recall the words that Agnes Ticher in her tipsiness had spoken, or ever now to retail the episode in the common-room; it was better not to dwell on any of it. They were, after all, friends and there could remain unspoken secrets between them. Every year between the mistral and the season they came to Bandol, and when they retired together to the bungalow they would continue to return. 'It is all second best,' said the voice of Agnes Ticher, but when Miss Grimshaw looked at her friend she knew that Miss Ticher had not spoken. Miss Grimshaw went away, jangling the shells in the yellow plastic bag and screening from her mind the thoughts that were attempting to invade it. There was a smell of garlic on the air, and from the kitchen came the rich odour of *soupe de poissons*, the favourite dish of both of them.

The Ballroom of Romance

On Sundays, or on Mondays if he couldn't make it and often he couldn't, Sunday being his busy day, Canon O'Connell arrived at the farm in order to hold a private service with Bridie's father, who couldn't get about any more, having had a leg amputated after gangrene had set in. They'd had a pony and cart then and Bridie's mother had been alive: it hadn't been difficult for the two of them to help her father on to the cart in order to make the journey to Mass. But two years later the pony had gone lame and eventually had to be destroyed; not long after that her mother had died. 'Don't worry about it at all,' Canon O'Connell had said, referring to the difficulty of transporting her father to Mass. 'I'll slip up by the week, Bridie.'

The milk lorry called daily for the single churn of milk, Mr. Driscoll delivered groceries and meal in his van, and took away the eggs that Bridie had collected during the week. Since Canon O'Connell had made his offer, in 1953, Bridie's father hadn't left the farm.

As well as Mass on Sundays and her weekly visits to a wayside dance-hall Bridie went shopping once every month, cycling to the town early on a Friday afternoon. She bought things for herself, material for a dress, knitting wool, stockings, a newspaper, and paper-backed Wild West novels for her father. She talked in the shops to some of the girls she'd been at school with, girls who had married shop-assistants or shop-keepers, or had become assistants themselves. Most of them had families of their own by now. 'You're lucky to be peaceful in the hills,' they said to Bridie, 'instead of stuck in a hole like this.' They had a tired look, most of them, from pregnancies and their efforts to organise and control their large families.

As she cycled back to the hills on a Friday Bridie often felt that they truly envied her her life, and she found it surprising that they should do so. If it hadn't been for her father she'd have wanted to work in the town also, in the tinned meat factory maybe, or in a shop. The town had a cinema called the Electric, and a fish-and-chip shop where people met at night, eating chips out of newspaper on the pavement outside. In the evenings, sitting in the farmhouse with her father, she often thought about the town, imagining the shop-windows lit up to display their goods and the sweet-shops still open so that people could purchase chocolates or fruit to take with them to the Electric cinema. But the town was eleven miles away, which was too far to cycle, there and back, for an evening's entertainment.

'It's a terrible thing for you, girl,' her father used to say, genuinely troubled, 'tied up to a one-legged man.' He would sigh heavily, hobbling back from the fields, where he managed as best he could. 'If your mother hadn't died,' he'd say, not finishing the sentence.

If her mother hadn't died her mother could have looked after him and the scant acres he owned, her mother could somehow have lifted the milk-churn on to the collection platform and attended to the few hens and the cows. 'I'd be dead without the girl to assist me,' she'd heard her father saying to Canon O'Connell, and Canon O'Connell replied that he was certainly lucky to have her.

'Amn't I as happy here as anywhere?' she'd say herself, but her father knew she was pretending and was saddened because the weight of circumstances had so harshly interfered with her life.

Although her father still called her a girl, Bridie was thirty-six. She was tall and strong: the skin of her fingers and her palms were stained and harsh to touch. The labour they'd experienced had found its way into them, as though juices had come out of vegetation and pigment out of soil: since childhood she'd torn away the rough scotch grass that grew each spring among her father's mangolds and sugar beet; since childhood she'd harvested potatoes in August, her hands daily rooting in the ground she loosened and turned. Wind had toughened the flesh of her face, sun had browned it; her neck and nose were lean, her lips touched with early wrinkles.

But on Saturday nights Bridie forgot the scotch grass and the soil. In different dresses she cycled to the dance-hall, encouraged to make the journey by her father. 'Doesn't it do you good, girl?' he'd say, as though he imagined she begrudged herself the pleasure. 'Why wouldn't you enjoy yourself?' She'd cook him his tea and then he'd settle down with the wireless, or maybe a Wild West novel. In time, while still she danced, he'd stoke the fire up and hobble his way upstairs to bed.

The dance-hall, owned by Mr. Justin Dwyer, was miles from anywhere, a lone building by the roadside with treeless boglands all around and a gravel expanse in front of it. On pink pebbled cement its title was painted in an azure blue that matched the depth of the background shade yet stood out well, unfussily proclaiming *The Ballroom of Romance*. Above these letters four coloured bulbs — in red, green, orange and mauve — were lit at appropriate times, an indication that the evening rendezvous was open for business. Only the façade of the building was pink, the other walls being a more ordinary grey. And inside, except for pink swing-doors, everything was blue.

On Saturday nights Mr. Justin Dwyer, a small, thin man, unlocked the metal grid that protected his property and drew it back, creating an open mouth from which music would later pour. He helped his wife to carry crates of lemonade and packets of biscuits from their car, and then took up a position in the tiny vestibule between the drawn-back grid and the pink swing-doors. He sat at a card-table, with money and tickets spread out before him. He'd made a fortune, people said: he owned other ballrooms also.

People came on bicycles or in old motor-cars, country people like Bridie from remote hill farms and villages. People who did not often see other people met there, girls and boys, men and women. They paid Mr. Dwyer and passed into his dance-hall, where shadows were cast on pale-blue walls and light from a crystal bowl was dim. The band, known as the Romantic Jazz Band, was composed of clarinet, drums and piano. The drummer sometimes sang.

Bridie had been going to the dance-hall since first she left the Presentation Nuns, before her mother's death. She didn't mind the journey, which was seven miles there and seven miles back: she'd travelled as far every day to the Presentation Nuns on the same bicycle, which had once been the property of her mother, an old Rudge purchased originally in 1936. On Sundays she cycled six miles to Mass, but she never minded either: she'd grown quite used to all that.

'How're you, Bridie?' inquired Mr. Justin Dwyer when she arrived in a new scarlet dress one autumn evening in 1971. She said she was all right and in reply to Mr. Dwyer's second query she said that her father was all right also. 'I'll go up one of these days,' promised Mr. Dwyer, which was a promise he'd been making for twenty years.

She paid the entrance fee and passed through the pink swing-doors. The Romantic Jazz Band was playing a familiar melody of the past, 'The Destiny Waltz'. In spite of the band's title, jazz was not ever played in the ballroom: Mr. Dwyer did not personally care for that kind of music, nor had he cared for various dance movements that had come and gone over the years. Jiving, rock and roll, twisting, and other such variations had all been resisted by Mr. Dwyer, who believed that a ballroom should be, as much as possible, a dignified place. The Romantic Jazz Band consisted of Mr. Maloney, Mr. Swanton, and Dano Ryan on drums. They were three middle-aged men who drove out from the town in Mr. Maloney's car, amateur performers who were employed otherwise by the tinned-meat factory, the Electricity Supply Board, and the County Council.

'How're you, Bridie?' inquired Dano Ryan as she passed him on her way to the cloakroom. He was idle for a moment with his drums, 'The Destiny Waltz' not calling for much attention from him.

'I'm all right, Dano,' she said. 'Are you fit yourself? Are the eyes better?' The week before he'd told her that he'd developed a watering of the eyes that must have been some kind of cold or other. He'd woken up with it in the morning and it had persisted until the afternoon: it was a new experience, he'd told her, adding that he'd never had a day's illness or discomfort in his life.

'I think I need glasses,' he said now, and as she passed into the cloakroom she imagined him in glasses, repairing the roads, as he was employed to do by the County Council. You hardly ever saw a road-mender with glasses, she reflected, and she wondered if all the dust that was inherent in his work had perhaps affected his eyes.

'How're you, Bridie?' a girl called Eenie Mackie said in the cloakroom, a girl who'd left the Presentation Nuns only a year ago.

'That's a lovely dress, Eenie,' Bridie said. 'Is it nylon, that?'

'Tricel actually. Drip-dry.'

Bridie took off her coat and hung it on a hook. There was a small wash-basin in the cloakroom above which hung a discoloured oval mirror. Used tissues and pieces of cotton-wool, cigarette-butts and matches covered the concrete floor. Lengths or green-painted timber partitioned off a lavatory in a corner.

'Jeez, you're looking great, Bridie,' Madge Dowding remarked, waiting for her turn at the mirror. She moved towards it as she spoke, taking off a pair of spectacles before endeavouring to apply make-up to the lashes of her eye. She stared myopically into the oval mirror, humming while the other girls became restive.

'Will you hurry up, for God's sake!' shouted Eenie

Mackie. 'We're standing here all night, Madge.'

Madge Dowding was the only one who was older than Bridie. She was thirty-nine, although often she said she was younger. The girls sniggered about that, saying that Madge Dowding should accept her condition — her age and her squint and her poor complexion — and not make herself ridiculous going out after men. What man would be bothered with the like of her anyway? Madge Dowding would do better to give herself over to do Saturday-night work for the Legion of Mary: wasn't Canon O'Connell always looking for aid?

'Is that fellow there?' she asked now, moving away from the mirror. 'The guy with the long arms. Did anyone see him outside?'

'He's dancing with Cat Bolger,' one of the girls replied. 'She has herself glued to him.'

'Lover boy,' remarked Patty Byrne, and everyone laughed because the person referred to was hardly a boy any more, being over fifty it was said, a bachelor who came only occasionally to the dance-hall.

Madge Dowding left the cloakroom rapidly, not bothering to pretend she wasn't anxious about the conjunction of Cat Bolger and the man with the long arms. Two sharp spots of red had come into her cheeks, and when she stumbled in her haste the girls in the cloakroom laughed. A younger girl would have pretended to be casual.

Bridie chatted, waiting for the mirror. Some girls, not wishing to be delayed, used the mirrors of their compacts. Then in twos and threes, occasionally singly, they left the cloakroom and took their places on upright wooden chairs at one end of the dance-hall, waiting to be asked to dance. Mr. Maloney, Mr. Swanton and Dano Ryan played 'Harvest Moon' and 'I Wonder Who's Kissing Her Now' and 'I'll Be Around'.

Bridie danced. Her father would be falling asleep by the fire; the wireless, tuned in to Radio Éireann, would be murmuring in the background. Already he'd have listened to *Faith and Order* and *Spot the Talent*. His Wild West novel, *Three Rode Fast* by Jake Matall, would have dropped from his single knee on to the flagged floor. He would wake with a jerk as he did every night and, forgetting what night it was, might be surprised not to see her, for usually she was sitting there at the table, mending clothes or washing eggs. 'Is it time for the News?' he'd automatically say.

Dust and cigarette smoke formed a haze beneath the crystal bowl, feet thudded, girls shrieked and laughed, some of them dancing together for want of a male partner. The music was loud, the musicians had taken off their jackets. Vigorously they played a number of tunes from *State Fair* and then, more romantically, 'Just One Of Those Things'. The tempo increased for a Paul Jones, after which Bridie found herself with a youth who told her he was saving up to emigrate, the nation in his opinion being finished. 'I'm up in the hills with the uncle,' he said, 'labouring fourteen hours a day. Is it any life for a young fellow?' She knew his uncle, a hill farmer whose stony acres were separated from her father's by one other farm only. 'He has me gutted with work,' the youth told her. 'Is there sense in it at all, Bridie?'

At ten o'clock there was a stir, occasioned by the arrival of three middle-aged bachelors who'd cycled over from Carey's public house. They shouted and whistled, greeting other people across the dancing area. They smelt of stout and sweat and whiskey.

Every Saturday at just this time they arrived, and, having sold them their tickets, Mr. Dwyer folded up his card-table and locked the tin box that held the evening's takings: his ballroom was complete.

'How're you, Bridie?' one of the bachelors, known as Bowser Egan, inquired. Another one, Tim Daly, asked Patty Byrne how she was. 'Will we take the floor?' Eyes Horgan suggested to Madge Dowding, already pressing the front of his navy-blue suit against the net of her dress. Bridie danced with Bowser Egan, who said she was looking great.

The bachelors would never marry, the girls of the dance-hall considered: they were wedded already, to stout and whiskey and laziness, to three old mothers somewhere up in the hills. The man with the long arms didn't drink but he was the same in all other ways: he had the same look of a bachelor, a quality in his face.

'Great,' Bowser Egan said, feather-stepping in an inaccurate and inebriated manner. 'You're a great little dancer, Bridie.'

'Will you lay off that!' cried Madge Dowding, her voice shrill above the sound of the music. Eyes Horgan had slipped two fingers into the back of her dress and was now pretending they'd got there by accident. He smiled blearily, his huge red face streaming with perspiration, the eyes which gave him his nickname protuberant and bloodshot.

'Watch your step with that one,' Bowser Egan called out, laughing so that spittle sprayed on to Bridie's face. Eenie Mackie, who was also dancing near the incident, laughed also and winked at Bridie. Dano Ryan left his drums and sang. 'Oh, how I miss your gentle kiss,' he crooned, 'and long to hold you tight.'

Nobody knew the name of the man with the long arms. The only words he'd ever been known to speak in the Ballroom of Romance were the words that formed his invitation to dance. He was a shy man who stood alone when he wasn't performing on the dance-floor. He rode away on his bicycle afterwards, not saying good night to anyone.

'Cat has your man leppin' tonight,' Tim Daly remarked to Patty Byrne, for the liveliness that Cat Bolger had introduced into foxtrot and waltz was noticeable.

'I think of you only,' sang Dano Ryan. 'Only wishing, wishing you were by my side.'

Dano Ryan would have done, Bridie often thought, because he was a different kind of bachelor: he had a lonely look about him, as if he'd become tired of being on his own. Every week she thought he would have done, and during the week her mind regularly returned to that thought. Dano Ryan would have done because she felt he wouldn't mind coming to live in the farmhouse while her one-legged father was still about the place. Three could live as cheaply as two where Dano Ryan was concerned because giving up the wages he earned as a road-worker would be balanced by the saving made on what he paid for lodgings. Once, at the end of an evening, she'd pretended that there was a puncture in the back wheel of her bicycle and he'd concerned himself with it while Mr. Maloney and Mr. Swanton waited for him in Mr. Maloney's car. He'd blown the tyre up with the car pump and had said he thought it would hold.

It was well known in the dance-hall that she fancied her chances with Dano Ryan. But it was well known also that Dano Ryan had got into a set way of life and had remained in it for quite some years. He lodged with a widow called Mrs. Griffin and Mrs. Griffin's mentally affected son, in a cottage on the outskirts of the town. He was said to be good to the affected child, buying him sweets and taking him out for rides on the cross-bar of his bicycle. He gave an hour or two of his time every week to the Church of Our Lady Queen of Heaven, and he was loyal to Mr. Dwyer. He performed in the two other rural dance-halls that Mr. Dwyer owned, rejecting advances from the town's more sophisticated dance-hall, even though it was more conveniently situated for him and the fee was more substantial than that paid by Mr. Dwyer. But Mr. Dwyer had discovered Dano Ryan and Dano had not forgotten it, just as Mr. Maloney and Mr. Swanton had not forgotten their discovery by Mr. Dwyer either.

'Would we take a lemonade?' Bowser Egan suggested. 'And a packet of biscuits, Bridie?'

No alcoholic liquor was ever served in the Ballroom of Romance, the premises not being licensed for this added stimulant. Mr. Dwyer in fact had never sought a licence for any of his premises, knowing that romance and alcohol were difficult commodities to mix, especially in a dignified ballroom. Behind where the girls sat on the wooden chairs

Mr. Dwyer's wife, a small stout woman, served the bottles of lemonade, with straws, and the biscuits and the crisps. She talked busily while doing so, mainly about the turkeys she kept. She'd once told Bridie that she thought of them as children.

'Thanks,' Bridie said, and Bowser Egan led her to the trestle table. Soon it would be intermission: soon the three members of the band would cross the floor also for refreshment. She thought up questions to ask Dano Ryan.

When first she'd danced in the Ballroom of Romance, when she was just sixteen, Dano Ryan had been there also, four years older than she was, playing the drums for Mr. Maloney as he played them now. She'd hardly noticed him then because of his not being one of the dancers: he was part of the ballroom's scenery, like the trestle table and the lemonade bottles, and Mrs. Dwyer and Mr. Dwyer. The youths who danced with her then in their Saturday-night blue suits had later disappeared into the town, or to Dublin or Britain, leaving behind them those who became the middle-aged bachelors of the hills. There'd been a boy called Patrick Grady whom she had loved in those days. Week after week she'd ridden away from the Ballroom of Romance with the image of his face in her mind, a thin face, pale beneath black hair. It had been different, dancing with Patrick Grady, and she'd felt that he found it different dancing with her, although he'd never said so. At night she'd dreamed of him and in the daytime too, while she helped her mother in the kitchen or her father with the cows. Week by week she'd returned to the ballroom, smiling on its pink façade and dancing then in the arms of Patrick Grady. Often they'd stood together drinking lemonade, not saying anything, not knowing what to say. She knew he loved her, and she believed then that he would lead her one day from the dim romantic ballroom, from its blueness and its pinkness and its crystal bowl of light and its music. She believed he would lead her into sunshine, to the town and the Church of Our Lady Queen of Heaven, to marriage and smiling faces. But someone else had got Patrick Grady, a girl from the town who'd never danced in the wayside ballroom. She'd scooped up Patrick Grady when he didn't have a chance.

Bridie had wept, hearing that. By night she'd lain in her bed in the farmhouse, quietly crying, the tears rolling into her hair and making the pillow damp. When she woke in the early morning the thought was still naggingly with her and it remained with her by day, replacing her daytime dreams of happiness. Someone told her later on that he'd crossed to Britain, to Wolverhampton, with the girl he'd married, and she imagined him there, in a place she wasn't able properly to visualise, labouring in a factory, his children being born and acquiring the accent of the area. The Ballroom of Romance wasn't the same without him, and when no one else stood out for her particularly over the years and when no one offered her marriage, she found herself wondering about Dano Ryan. If you couldn't have love, the next best thing was surely a decent man.

Bowser Egan hardly fell into that category, nor did Tim Daly. And it was plain to everyone that Cat Bolger and Madge Dowding were wasting their time over the man with the long arms. Madge Dowding was already a figure of fun in the ballroom, the way she ran after the bachelors; Cat Bolger would end up the same if she wasn't careful. One way or another it wasn't difficult to be a figure of fun in the ballroom, and you didn't have to be as old as Madge Dowding: a girl who'd just left the Presentation Nuns had once asked Eyes Horgan what he had in his trouser pocket and he told her it was a penknife. She'd repeated this afterwards in the cloakroom, how she'd requested Eyes Horgan not to dance so close to her because his penknife was sticking into her. 'Jeez, aren't you the right baby!' Patty Byrne had shouted delightedly: everyone had laughed, knowing that Eyes Horgan only came to the ballroom for stuff like that. He was no use to any girl.

'Two lemonades, Mrs. Dwyer,' Bowser Egan said, 'and two packets of Kerry Creams. Is Kerry Creams all right,

Bridie?'

She nodded, smiling. Kerry Creams would be fine, she said.

'Well, Bridie, isn't that the great outfit you have!' Mrs. Dwyer remarked. 'Doesn't the red suit her, Bowser?'

By the swing-doors stood Mr. Dwyer, smoking a cigarette that he held cupped in his left hand. His small eyes noted all developments. He had been aware of Madge Dowding's anxiety when Eyes Horgan had inserted two fingers into the back opening of her dress. He had looked away, not caring for the incident, but had it developed further he would have spoken to Eyes Horgan, as he had on other occasions. Some of the younger lads didn't know any better and would dance very close to their partners, who generally were too embarrassed to do anything about it, being young themselves. But that, in Mr. Dwyer's opinion, was a different kettle of fish altogether because they were decent young lads who'd in no time at all be doing a steady line with a girl and would end up as he had himself with Mrs. Dwyer, in the same house with her, sleeping in a bed with her, firmly married. It was the middle-aged bachelors who required the watching: they came down from the hills like mountain goats, released from their mammies and from the smell of animals and soil. Mr. Dwyer continued to watch Eyes Horgan, wondering how drunk he was.

Dano Ryan's song came to an end, Mr. Swanton laid down his clarinet, Mr. Maloney rose from the piano. Dano Ryan wiped sweat from his face and the three men slowly moved towards Mrs. Dwyer's trestle table.

'Jeez, you have powerful legs,' Eyes Horgan whispered to Madge Dowding, but Madge Dowding's attention was on the man with the long arms, who had left Cat Bolger's side and was proceeding in the direction of the men's lavatory. He never took refreshments. She moved, herself, towards the men's lavatory, to take up a position outside it, but Eyes Horgan followed her. 'Would you take a lemonade, Madge?' he asked. He had a small bottle of whiskey on him: if they went into a corner they could add a drop of it to the lemonade. She didn't drink spirits, she reminded him, and he went away.

'Excuse me a minute,' Bowser Egan said, putting down his bottle of lemonade. He crossed the floor to the lavatory. He too, Bridie knew, would have a small bottle of whiskey on him. She watched while Dano Ryan, listening to a story Mr. Maloney was telling, paused in the centre of the ballroom, his head bent to hear what was being said. He was a big man, heavily made, with black hair that was slightly touched with grey, and big hands. He laughed when Mr. Maloney came to the end of his story and then bent his head again, in order to listen to a story told by Mr. Swanton.

'Are you on your own, Bridie?' Cat Bolger asked, and Bridie said she was waiting for Bowser Egan. 'I think I'll have a lemonade,' Cat Bolger said.

Younger boys and girls stood with their arms still around one another, queueing up for refreshments. Boys who hadn't danced at all, being nervous because they didn't know any steps, stood in groups, smoking and making jokes. Girls who hadn't been danced with yet talked to one another, their eyes wandering. Some of them sucked their straws in lemonade bottles.

Bridie, still watching Dano Ryan, imagined him wearing the glasses he'd referred to, sitting in the farmhouse kitchen, reading one of her father's Wild West novels. She imagined the three of them eating a meal she'd prepared, fried eggs and rashers and fried potato-cakes and tea and bread and butter and jam, brown bread and soda and shop bread. She imagined Dano Ryan leaving the kitchen in the morning to go out to the fields in order to weed the mangolds, and her father hobbling off behind him, and the two men working together. She saw hay being cut, Dano Ryan with the scythe that she'd learned to use herself, her father using a rake as best he could. She saw herself, because of the extra help, being able to attend to things in the farmhouse, things she'd never had time for because of the cows and the hens and the fields. There were bedroom curtains that needed repairing where the net had ripped, and wallpaper that had become loose and needed to be stuck up with flour paste. The scullery required whitewashing.

The night he'd blown up the tyre of her bicycle she'd thought he was going to kiss her. He'd crouched on the ground in the darkness with his ear to the tyre, listening for escaping air. When he could hear none he'd straightened up and said he thought she'd be all right on the bicycle. His face had been quite close to hers and she'd smiled at him. At that moment, unfortunately, Mr. Maloney had blown an impatient blast on the horn of his motor-car.

Often she'd been kissed by Bowser Egan, on the nights when he insisted on riding part of the way home with her. They had to dismount in order to push their bicycles up a hill and the first time he'd accompanied her he'd contrived to fall against her, steadying himself by putting a hand on her shoulder. The next thing she was aware of was the moist quality of his lips and the sound of his bicycle as it clattered noisily on the road. He'd suggested then, regaining his breath, that they should go into a field.

That was nine years ago. In the intervening passage of time she'd been kissed as well, in similar circumstances, by Eyes Horgan and Tim Daly. She'd gone into fields with them and permitted them to put their arms about her while heavily they breathed. At one time or another she had imagined marriage with one or other of them, seeing them in the farmhouse with her father, even though the fantasies were unlikely.

Bridie stood with Cat Bolger, knowing that it would be some time before Bowser Egan came out of the lavatory. Mr. Maloney, Mr. Swanton and Dano Ryan approached, Mr. Maloney insisting that he would fetch three bottles of lemonade from the trestle table.

'You sang the last one beautifully,' Bridie said to Dano Ryan. 'Isn't it a beautiful song?'

Mr. Swanton said it was the finest song ever written, and Cat Bolger said she preferred 'Danny Boy', which in her opinion was the finest song ever written.

'Take a suck of that,' said Mr. Maloney, handing Dano Ryan and Mr. Swanton bottles of lemonade. 'How's Bridie tonight? Is your father well, Bridie?'

Her father was all right, she said.

'I hear they're starting a cement factory,' said Mr. Maloney. 'Did anyone hear talk of that? They're after striking some commodity in the earth that makes good cement. Ten feet down, over at Kilmalough."

'It'll bring employment," said Mr. Swanton. 'It's employment that's necessary in this area.'

'Canon O'Connell was on about it,' Mr. Maloney said. 'There's Yankee money involved.'

'Will the Yanks come over?' inquired Cat Bolger. 'Will they run it themselves, Mr. Maloney?'

Mr. Maloney, intent on his lemonade, didn't hear the questions and Cat Bolger didn't repeat them.

'There's stuff called Optrex,' Bridie said quietly to Dano Ryan, 'that my father took the time he had a cold in his eyes. Maybe Optrex would settle the watering, Dano.'

'Ah sure, it doesn't worry me that much –'

'It's terrible, anything wrong with the eyes. You wouldn't want to take a chance. You'd get Optrex in a chemist, Dano, and a little bowl with it so that you can bathe the eyes.'

Her father's eyes had become red-rimmed and unsightly to look at. She'd gone into Riordan's Medical Hall in the town and had explained what the trouble was, and Mr. Riordan had recommended Optrex. She told this to Dano Ryan, adding that her father had had no trouble with his eyes since. Dano Ryan nodded.

'Did you hear that, Mrs. Dwyer?' Mr. Maloney called out. 'A cement factory for Kilmalough.'

Mrs Dwyer wagged her head, placing empty bottles in a crate. She'd heard references to the cement factory, she said: it was the best news for a long time.

'Kilmalough'll never know itself,' her husband commented, joining her in her task with the empty lemonade bottles.

' 'Twill bring prosperity certainly,' said Mr. Swanton. 'I was saying just there, Justin, that employment's what's necessary.'

'Sure, won't the Yanks –' began Cat Bolger, but Mr. Maloney interrupted her.

'The Yanks'll be in at the top, Cat, or maybe not here at all – maybe only inserting money into it. It'll be local labour entirely.'

'You'll not marry a Yank, Cat,' said Mr. Swanton, loudly laughing. 'You can't catch those fellows.'

'Haven't you plenty of homemade bachelors?' suggested Mr. Maloney. He laughed also, throwing away the straw he was sucking through and tipping the bottle into his mouth. Cat Bolger told him to get on with himself. She moved towards the men's lavatory and took up a position outside it, not speaking to Madge Dowding, who was still standing there.

'Keep a watch on Eyes Horgan,' Mrs. Dwyer warned her husband, which was advice she gave him at this time every Saturday night, knowing that Eyes Horgan was drinking in the lavatory. When he was drunk Eyes Horgan was the most difficult of the bachelors.

'I have a drop of it left, Dano,' Bridie said quietly. 'I could bring it over on Saturday. The eye stuff.'

'Ah, don't worry yourself, Bridie –'

'No trouble at all. Honestly now –'

'Mrs. Griffin has me fixed up for a test with Dr. Cready. The old eyes are no worry, only when I'm reading the paper or at the pictures. Mrs. Griffin says I'm only straining them due to lack of glasses.'

He looked away while he said that, and she knew at once that Mrs. Griffin was arranging to marry him. She felt it instinctively: Mrs. Griffin was going to marry him because she was afraid that if he moved away from her cottage, to get married to someone else, she'd find it hard to replace him with another lodger who'd be good to her affected son. He'd become a father to Mrs. Griffin's affected son, to whom already he was kind. It was a natural outcome, for Mrs. Griffin had all the chances, seeing him every night and morning and not having to make do with weekly encounters in a ballroom.

She thought of Patrick Grady, seeing in her mind his pale, thin face. She might be the mother of four of his children now, or seven or eight maybe. She might be living in Wolverhampton, going out to the pictures in the evenings, instead of looking after a one-legged man. If the weight of circumstances hadn't intervened she wouldn't be standing in a wayside ballroom, mourning the marriage of a road-mender she didn't love. For a moment she thought she might cry, standing there thinking of Patrick Grady in Wolverhampton. In her life, on the farm and in the house, there was no place for tears. Tears were a luxury, like flowers would be in the fields where the mangolds grew, or fresh whitewash in the scullery. It wouldn't have been fair ever to have wept in the kitchen while her father sat listening to *Spot the Talent*: her father had more right to weep, having lost a leg. He suffered in a greater way, yet he remained kind and concerned for her.

In the Ballroom of Romance she felt behind her eyes the tears that it would have been improper to release in the presence of her father. She wanted to let them go, to feel them streaming on her cheeks, to receive the sympathy of Dano Ryan and of everyone else. She wanted them all to listen to her while she told them about Patrick Grady who was now in Wolverhampton and about the death of her mother and her own life since. She wanted Dano Ryan to put his arm around her so that she could lean her head against it. She wanted him to look at her in his decent way and to stroke with his road-mender's fingers the backs of her hands. She might wake in a bed with him and imagine for a moment that he was Patrick Grady. She might bathe his eyes and pretend.

'Back to business,' said Mr. Maloney, leading his band

55

across the floor to their instruments.

'Tell your father I was asking for him,' Dano Ryan said. She smiled and she promised, as though nothing had happened, that she would tell her father that.

She danced with Tim Daly and then again with the youth who'd said he intended to emigrate. She saw Madge Dowding moving swiftly towards the man with the long arms as he came out of the lavatory, moving faster than Cat Bolger. Eyes Horgan approached Cat Bolger. Dancing with her, he spoke earnestly, attempting to persuade her to permit him to ride part of the way home with her. He was unaware of the jealousy that was coming from her as she watched Madge Dowding holding close to her the man with the long arms while they performed a quickstep. Cat Bolger was in her thirties too.

'Get away out of that,' said Bowser Egan, cutting in on the youth who was dancing with Bridie. 'Go home to your mammy, boy.' He took her into his arms, saying again that she was looking great tonight. 'Did you hear about the cement factory?' he said 'Isn't it great for Kilmalough?'

She agreed. She said what Mr. Swanton and Mr. Maloney had said: that the cement factory would bring employment to the neighbourhood.

'Will I ride home with you a bit, Bridie?' Bowser Egan suggested, and she pretended not to hear him. 'Aren't you my girl, Bridie, and always have been?' he said, a statement that made no sense at all.

His voice went on whispering at her, saying he would marry her tomorrow only his mother wouldn't permit another woman in the house. She knew what it was like herself, he reminded her, having a parent to look after: you couldn't leave them to rot, you had to honour your father and your mother.

She danced to 'The Bells Are Ringing', moving her legs in time with Bowser Egan's while over his shoulder she watched Dano Ryan softly striking one of his smaller drums. Mrs. Griffin had got him even though she was nearly fifty, with no looks at all, a lumpish woman with lumpish legs and arms. Mrs. Griffin had got him just as the girl had got Patrick Grady.

The music ceased, Bowser Egan held her hard against him, trying to touch her face with his. Around them, people whistled and clapped: the evening had come to an end. She walked away from Bowser Egan, knowing that not ever again would she dance in the Ballroom of Romance. She'd been a figure of fun, trying to promote a relationship with a middle-aged County Council labourer, as ridiculous as Madge Dowding dancing on beyond her time.

'I'm waiting outside for you, Cat,' Eyes Horgan called out, lighting a cigarette as he made for the swing-doors.

Already the man with the long arms — made long, so they said, from carrying rocks off his land — had left the ballroom. Others were moving briskly. Mr. Dwyer was tidying the chairs.

In the cloakroom the girls put on their coats and said they'd see one another at Mass the next day. Madge Dowding hurried. 'Are you O.K., Bridie?' Patty Byrne asked and Bridie said she was. She smiled at little Patty Byrne, wondering if a day would come for the younger girl also, if one day she'd decide that she was a figure of fun in a wayside ballroom.

'Good night so,' Bridie said, leaving the cloakroom, and the girls who were still chatting there wished her good night. Outside the cloakroom she paused for a moment. Mr. Dwyer was still tidying the chairs, picking up empty lemonade bottles from the floor, setting the chairs in a neat row. His wife was sweeping the floor. 'Good night, Bridie,' Mr. Dwyer said, 'Good night, Bridie,' his wife said.

Extra lights had been switched on so that the Dwyers could see what they were doing. In the glare the blue walls of the ballroom seemed tatty, marked with hair-oil where men had leaned against them, inscribed with names and initials and hearts with arrows through them. The crystal bowl gave out a light that was ineffective in the glare, the bowl was broken here and there, which wasn't noticeable when the other lights weren't on.

'Good night so,' Bridie said to the Dwyers. She passed through the swing-doors and descended the three concrete steps on the gravel expanse in front of the ballroom. People were gathered on the gravel, talking in groups, standing with their bicycles. She saw Madge Dowding going off with Tim Daly. A youth rode away with a girl on the cross-bar of his bicycle. The engines of motor-cars started.

'Good night, Bridie,' Dano Ryan said.

'Good night, Dano,' she said.

She walked across the gravel towards her bicycle, hearing Mr. Maloney, somewhere behind her, repeating that no matter how you looked at it the cement factory would be a great thing for Kilmalough. She heard the bang of a car-door and knew it was Mr. Swanton banging the door of Mr. Maloney's car because he always gave it the same loud bang. Two other doors banged as she reached her bicycle and then the engines started up and the headlights went on. She touched the two tyres of the bicycle to make certain she hadn't a puncture. The wheels of Mr. Maloney's car traversed the gravel and were silent when they reached the road.

'Good night, Bridie,' someone called, and she replied, pushing her bicycle towards the road.

'Will I ride a little way with you?' Bowser Egan asked.

They rode together and when they arrived at the hill for which it was necessary to dismount she looked back and saw in the distance the four coloured bulbs that decorated the facade of the Ballroom of Romance. As she watched the lights went out, and she imagined Mr. Dwyer pulling the metal grid across the front of his property and locking the two padlocks that secured it. His wife would be waiting with the evening's takings, sitting in the front of their car.

'D'you know what it is, Bridie,' said Bowser Egan, 'you

were never looking better than tonight.' He took from a pocket of his suit the small bottle of whiskey he had. He uncorked it and drank some and then handed it to her. She took it and drank, 'Sure, why wouldn't you?' he said, surprised to see her drinking because she never had in his company before. It was an unpleasant taste, she considered, a taste she'd experienced only twice before, when she'd taken whiskey as a remedy for toothache. 'What harm would it do you?' Bowser Egan said as she raised the bottle again to her lips. He reached out a hand for it, though, suddenly concerned lest she should consume a greater share than he wished her to.

She watched him drinking more expertly that she had. He would always be drinking, she thought. He'd be lazy and useless, sitting in the kitchen with the *Irish Press*. He'd waste money buying a second-hand motor-car in order to drive into the town to go to the public houses on fair-days.

'She's shook these days,' he said, referring to his mother. 'She'll hardly last two years, I'm thinking.' He threw the empty whiskey bottle into the ditch and lit a cigarette. They pushed their bicycles. He said:

'When she goes, Bridie, I'll sell the bloody place up. I'll sell the pigs and the whole damn one and twopence worth.' He paused in order to raise the cigarette to his lips. He drew in smoke and exhaled it. 'With the cash that I'll get I could improve some place else, Bridie.'

They reached a gate on the left-hand side of the road and automatically they pushed their bicycles towards it and leaned them against it. He climbed over the gate into the field and she climbed after him. 'Will we sit down here, Bridie?' he said, offering the suggestion as one that had just occured to him, as though they'd entered the field for some other purpose.

'We could improve a place like your own one,' he said, putting his right arm around her shoulders. 'Have you a kiss in you, Bridie?' He kissed her, exerting pressure with his teeth. When his mother died he would sell his farm and spend the money in the town. After that he would think of

59

getting married because he'd have nowhere to go, because he'd want a fire to sit at and a woman to cook food for him. He kissed her again, his lips hot, the sweat on his cheeks sticking to her. 'God, you're great at kissing,' he said.

She rose, saying it was time to go, and they climbed over the gate again. 'There's nothing like a Saturday,' he said. 'Good night to you so, Bridie.'

He mounted his bicycle and rode down the hill, and she pushed hers to the top and then mounted it also. She rode through the night as on Saturday nights for years she had ridden and never would ride again because she'd reached a certain age. She would wait now and in time Bowser Egan would seek her out because his mother would have died. Her father would probably have died also by then. She would marry Bowser Egan because it would be lonesome being by herself in the farmhouse.

The Distant Past

In the town and beyond it they were regarded as harmlessly peculiar. Odd, people said, and in time this reference took on a burnish of affection.

They had always been thin, silent with one another, and similar in appearance: a brother and sister who shared a family face. It was a bony countenance, with pale blue eyes and a sharp, well-shaped nose and high cheek-bones. Their father had had it too, but unlike them their father had been an irresponsible and careless man, with red flecks in his cheeks that they didn't have at all. The Middletons of Carraveagh the family had once been known as, but now the brother and sister were just the Middletons, for Carraveagh didn't count any more, except to them.

They owned four Herefords, a number of hens, and the house itself, three miles outside the town. It was a large house, built in the reign of George II, a monument that reflected in its glory and later decay the fortunes of a family. As the brother and sister aged, its roof increasingly ceased to afford protection, rust ate at its gutters, grass thrived in two thick channels all along its avenue. Their father had mortgaged his inherited estate, so local rumour claimed, in order to keep a Catholic Dublin woman in brandy and jewels. When he died in 1924, his two children discovered that they possessed only a dozen acres. It was locally said also that this adversity hardened their will and that because of it they came to love the remains of Carraveagh more than they could ever have loved a husband or a wife. They blamed for their ill-fortune the Catholic Dublin woman whom they'd never met and they blamed as well the new national régime, contriving in their eccentric way to relate the two. In the days of the Union Jack such women would have known their place: wasn't it all part and parcel?

Twice a week, on Fridays and Sundays, the Middletons journeyed into the town, first of all in a trap and later in a Ford Anglia car. In the shops and elsewhere they made, quite gently, no secret of their continuing loyalty to the past. They attended on Sundays St. Patrick's Protestant Church, a place that matched their mood, for prayers were still said there for the King whose sovereignty their country had denied. The revolutionary régime would not last, they quietly informed the Reverend Packham: what sense was there in green-painted pillar-boxes and a language that nobody understood?

On Fridays, when they took seven or eight dozen eggs to the town, they dressed in pressed tweeds and were accompanied over the years by a series of red setters, the breed there had always been at Carraveagh. They sold the eggs in Keogh's grocery and then had a drink with Mrs. Keogh in the part of her shop that was devoted to the consumption of refreshment. Mr. Middleton had whiskey and his sister Tio Pepe. They enjoyed the occasion, for they liked Mrs. Keogh and they were liked by her in return. Afterwards they shopped, chatting to the shopkeepers about whatever news there was, and then they went to Healy's Hotel for a few more drinks before driving home.

Drink was their pleasure and it was through it that they built up, in spite of their loyalty to the past, such convivial relationships with the people of the town. Fat Driscoll, who kept the butcher's shop, used even to joke about the past when he stood with them in Healy's Hotel or stood behind his own counter cutting their slender chops or thinly slicing their liver. 'Will you ever forget it, Mr. Middleton! I'd ha' run like a rabbit if you'd lifted a finger at me.' Fat Driscoll would laugh then, rocking back on his heels with a glass of stout in his hand or banging their meat on to his weighing-scales. Mr. Middleton would smile. 'There was alarm in your eyes, Mr. Driscoll,' Miss Middleton would murmur, smiling also at the memory of the distant occasion.

Fat Driscoll, with a farmer called Maguire and another called Breen, had stood in the hall of Carraveagh, each of them in charge of a shot-gun. The Middletons, children then, had been locked with their mother and father and an aunt into an upstairs room. Nothing else had happened: the expected British soldiers had not, after all, arrived and the men in the hall had eventually relaxed their vigil. 'A massacre they wanted,' the Middletons' father said after they'd gone. 'Damn bloody ruffians.'

The Second World War took place. Two Germans, a man and his wife called Winkelmann who ran a glove factory in the town, were suspected by the Middletons of being spies for the Third Reich. People laughed, for they knew the Winkelmanns well and could lend no credence to the Middletons' latest fantasy: typical of them, they explained to the Winkelmanns, who had been worried.

Soon after the War the Reverend Packham died and was replaced by the Reverend Hosford, a younger man who laughed also and regarded the Middletons as an anachronism. They protested when prayers were no longer said for the Royal Family in St. Patrick's but the Reverend Hosford considered that their protests were as absurd as the prayers themselves had been. Why pray for the monarchy of a neighbouring island when their own island had its chosen President now? The Middletons didn't reply to that argument. In the Reverend Hosford's presence they rose to their feet when the BBC played God Save the King, and on the day of the coronation of Queen Elizabeth II they drove into the town with a small Union Jack propped up in the back window of their Ford Anglia. 'Bedad, you're a holy terror, Mr. Middleton!' Fat Driscoll laughingly exclaimed, noticing the flag as he lifted a tray of pork-steaks from his display shelf. The Middletons smiled. It was a great day for the Commonwealth of Nations, they replied, a remark which further amused Fat Driscoll and which he later repeated in Phelan's public house. 'Her Britannic Majesty' guffawed his friend Mr. Breen.

Situated in a valley that was noted for its beauty and with convenient access to rich rivers and bogs over which game-birds flew, the town benefited from post-war tourism. Healy's Hotel changed its title and became, overnight, the New Ormonde. Shopkeepers had their shopfronts painted and Mr. Healy organised an annual Salmon Festival. Canon Kelly, who had at first commented severely on the habits of the tourists, and in particular on the summertime dress of the women, was in the end obliged to confess that the morals of his flock remained unaffected. 'God and good sense,' he proclaimed, meaning God and his own teaching. In time he even derived pride from the fact that people with other values came briefly to the town and that the values esteemed by his parishioners were in no way diminished.

The town's grocers now stocked foreign cheeses, Brie and Camembert and Port Salut, and wines were available to go with them. The plush Cocktail Room of the New Ormonde set a standard: the wife of a solicitor, a Mrs. O'Brien, began to give six o'clock parties once or twice a year, obliging her husband to mix gin and Martini in glass jugs and handing round herself a selection of nuts and small Japanese crackers. Canon Kelly looked in as a rule and satisfied himself that all was above board. He rejected, though, the mixture in the jugs, retaining his taste for a glass of John Jameson.

From the windows of their convent the Loreto nuns observed the long sleek cars with GB plates and English and American accents drifted on the breeze to them. Mothers cleaned up their children and sent them to the Golf Club to seek employment as caddies. Sweet shops sold holiday memories. The brown, soda and currant breads of Murphy-Floods's bakery were declared to be delicious. Mr. Healy doubled the number of local girls who served as waitresses in his dining-room, and in the winter of 1961 he had the builders in again, working on an extension for which the Munster and Leinster Bank had lent him £22,000.

But as the town increased its prosperity Carraveagh continued its decline. The Middletons were in their middle-sixties now and were reconciled to a life that became more uncomfortable with every passing year. Together they roved the vast lofts of their house, placing old paint tins and flower-pot saucers beneath the drips from the roof. At night they sat over their thin chops in a dining-room that had once been gracious and which in a way was gracious still, except for the faded appearance of furniture that was dry from lack of polish and of wallpaper that time had rendered colourless. In the hall their father gazed down at them, framed in ebony and gilt, in the uniform of the Irish Guards. He had conversed with Queen Victoria and even in their middle-sixties they could still hear him saying that God and Empire and Queen formed a trinity unique in any worthy soldier's heart. In the hall hung the family crest, and on ancient Irish linen the Cross of St. George.

The dog that accompanied the Middletons now was called Turloch, an animal whose death they dreaded for they felt they couldn't manage the antics of another pup. Turloch, being 13, moved slowly and was blind and a little deaf. He was a reminder, to them of their own advancing years and of the effort it had become to tend the Herefords and collect the weekly eggs. More and more they looked forward to Fridays, to the warm companionship of Mrs. Keogh and Mr. Healy's chatter in the hotel. They stayed longer now with Mrs. Keogh and in the hotel, and idled longer in the shops, and drove home more slowly. Dimly, but with no less loyalty, they still recalled the distant past and were listened to without ill-feeling when they spoke of it and of Carraveagh as it had been, and of the Queen whose company their careless father had known.

The visitors who came to the town heard about the Middletons and were impressed. It was a pleasant wonder, more than one of them remarked that old wounds could heal so completely, that the Middletons continued in their loyalty to the past and that in spite of it, they were respected in the town. When Miss Middleton had been ill with a form of pneumonia in 1958 Canon Kelly had driven out to Carraveagh twice a week with pullets and young ducks that his housekeeper had dressed. 'An upright couple,' was the Canon's public opinion of the Middletons and he had been known to add that eccentric views would hurt you less than malice. 'We can disagree without guns in this town,' Mr. Healy pronounced in his Cocktail Room, and his visitors usually replied that as far as they could see that was the result of living in a Christian country. That the Middletons bought their meat from a man who had once locked them into an upstairs room and had then waited to shoot soldiers in their hall was a fact that amazed the seasonal visitors. You lived and learned, they remarked to Mr. Healy.

The Middletons, privately, often considered that they led a strange life. Alone in their beds at night they now and again wondered why they hadn't just sold Carraveagh forty-eight years ago when their father had died: why had the tie been so strong and why had they in perversity encouraged it? They didn't fully know, nor did they attempt to discuss the matter in any way. Instinctively they had remained at Carraveagh, instinctively feeling that it would have been cowardly to go. Yet often it seemed to them now to be no more than a game they played, this worship of the distant past. And at other times it seemed as real and as important as the remaining acres of land, and the house itself.

'Isn't that shocking?' Mr. Healy said one day in 1967. 'Did you hear about that, Mr. Middleton, blowing up them post offices in Belfast?'

Mr. Healy, red-faced and short-haired, spoke casually in his Cocktail Lounge, making midday conversation. He had commented in much the same way at breakfasttime, looking up from the *Irish Independent*. Everyone in the town had said it too: that the blowing up of sub-post offices in

Belfast was a shocking matter.

'A bad business,' Fat Driscoll remarked, wrapping the Middletons' meat. 'We don't want that old stuff all over again.'

'We didn't want it in the first place,' Miss Middleton reminded him. He laughed, and she laughed, and so did her brother. Yes, it was a game, she thought: how could any of it be as real or as important as the afflictions and problems of the old butcher himself, his rheumatism and his reluctance to retire? Did her brother, she wondered, privately think so too?

'Come on, old Turloch,' he said, stroking the flank of the red setter with the point of his shoe, and she reflected that you could never tell what he was thinking. Certainly it wasn't the kind of thing you wanted to talk about.

'I've put him in a bit of mince,' Fat Driscoll said, which was something he often did these days, pretending the mince would otherwise be thrown away. There'd been a red setter about the place that night, when he waited in the hall for the soldiers: Breen and Maguire had pushed it down into a cellar, frightened of it.

'There's a heart of gold in you, Mr. Driscoll,' Miss Middleton murmured, nodding and smiling at him. He was the same age as she was, 66: he should have shut up shop years ago. He would have, he'd once told them, if there'd been a son to leave the business to. As it was he'd have to sell it and when it came to the point he found it hard to make the necessary arrangements. 'Like us and Carraveagh,' she'd said, even though on the face of it it didn't seem the same at all.

Every evening they sat in the big old kitchen, hearing the news. It was only in Belfast and Derry, the wireless said: outside Belfast and Derry you wouldn't know anything was happening at all. On Fridays they listened to the talk, in Mrs. Keogh's bar and in the hotel. 'Well, thank God it has nothing to do with the South,' Mr. Healy said often, usually repeating the statement.

The first British soldiers landed in the North of Ireland,

and soon people didn't so often say that outside Belfast and Derry you wouldn't know anything was happening. There were incidents in Fermanagh and Armagh, in Border villages and towns. One Prime Minister resigned and then another one. The troops were unpopular, the newspapers said; internment became part of the machinery of government. In the town, in St. Patrick's Protestant Church and in the Church of the Holy Assumption, prayers were offered, but no peace came.

'We're hit, Mr. Middleton,' Mr. Healy said one Friday morning. 'If there's a dozen visitors this summer it'll be God's own stroke of luck for us.'

'Luck?'

'Sure, who wants to come to a country with all that mularkey in it?'

'But, it's only the North.'

'Tell that to your tourists, Mr. Middleton.'

The town's prosperity ebbed. The Border was more than 60 miles away, but over that distance had spread some wisps of the fog of war. As anger rose in the town at the loss of fortunes so there rose also the kind of talk there had been in the distant past. There was talk of atrocities and counter-atrocities, and of guns and gelignite and the rights of people. There was bitterness suddenly in Mrs. Keogh's bar because of the lack of trade, and in the empty hotel there was bitterness also.

On Fridays, only sometimes at first, there was a silence when the Middletons appeared. It was as though, going back nearly twenty year, people remembered the Union Jack in the window of their car and saw it now in a different light. It wasn't something to laugh at any more, nor were certain words that the Middletons had gently spoken, nor were they themselves just an old peculiar couple. Slowly the change crept about, all around them in the town, until Fat Driscoll didn't wish it to be remembered that he had ever given them mince for their dog. He had stood with a gun in the enemy's house, waiting for soldiers so that soldiers might be killed: it was better that people should remember that.

One day Canon Kelly looked the other way when he saw the Middletons' car coming and they noticed this movement of his head, although he hadn't wished them to. And on another day Mrs. O'Brien, who had always been keen to talk to them in the hotel, didn't reply when they addressed her.

The Middletons naturally didn't discuss these rebuffs but they each of them privately knew that there was no conversation they could have at this time with the people of the town. the stand they had taken and kept to for so many years no longer seemed ridiculous in the town. Had they driven with a Union Jack now they would, astoundingly, have been shot.

'It will never cease.' He spoke disconsolately one night, standing by the dresser where the wireless was.

She washed the dishes they'd eaten from, and the cutlery. 'Not in our time,' she said.

'It is worse than before.'

'Yes, it is worse than before.'

They took from the walls of the hall the portrait of their father in the uniform of the Irish Guards because it seemed wrong to them that at this time it should hang there. They took down also the crest of their family and the Cross of St. George, and from the vase on the drawingroom mantelpiece they removed the small Union Jack that had been there since the Coronation of Queen Elizabeth II. They did not remove these articles in fear but in mourning for the *modus vivendi* that had existed for so long between them and the people of the town. They had given their custom to a butcher who had planned to shoot down soldiers in their hall, and he in turn had given them mince for their dog. For fifty years they had experienced, after suspicion had seeped away, a tolerance that never again in the years that were left to them would they know.

One November night their dog died and he said to her after he had buried it that they must not be depressed by all that was happening. They would die themselves and the house would become a ruin because there was no one to inherit it, and the distant past would be set to rest. But she disagreed: the *modus vivendi* had been easy for them, she pointed out, because they hadn't really minded the dwindling of their fortunes while the town prospered. It had given them a life, and a kind of dignity: you could take a pride out of living in peace.

He did not say anything and, then, because of the emotion that both of them felt over the death of their dog, he said in a rushing way that they could no longer at their age hope to make a living out of the remains of Carraveagh. They must sell the hens and the four Herefords, and as he spoke he watched her nodding, agreeing with the sense of it. Now and again, he thought, he would drive slowly in to the town to buy groceries and meat with the money they had saved, and to face the silence that would sourly thicken as their own two deaths came closer and death increased in another part of of their island. She felt him thinking that and she knew that he was right. Because of the distant past they would die friendless. It was worse than being murdered in their beds.

Death in Jerusalem

'Till then,' Father Paul said, leaning out of the train window. 'Till Jerusalem, Francis.'

'Please God, Paul.' As he spoke the Dublin train began to move and his brother waved from the window and he waved back, a modest figure on the platform. Everyone said Francis might have been a priest as well, meaning that Francis's quietness and meditative disposition had an air of the cloister about them. But Francis contented himself with the running of Daly's hardware business which his mother had run until she was too old for it. 'Are we game for the Holy Land next year?' Father Paul had asked that July. 'Will we go together, Francis?' He had brushed aside all Francis's protestations, all attempts to explain that the shop could not be left, that their mother would be confused by the absence of Francis from the house. Rumbustiously he'd pointed out that there was their sister Kitty, who was in charge of the household of which Francis and their mother were part and whose husband Myles could surely be trusted to look after the shop for a single fortnight. For thirty years, ever since he was seven, Francis had wanted to go to the Holy Land. He had savings which he'd never spent a penny of: you couldn't take them with you, Father Paul had more than once stated that July.

On the platform Francis watched until the train could no longer be seen, his thoughts still with his brother. The priest's ruddy countenance smiled again behind cigarette smoke; his bulk remained impressive in his clerical clothes, the collar pinching the flesh of his neck, his black shoes scrupulously polished. There were freckles on the backs of his large, strong hands; he had a fine head of hair, grey and crinkly. In an hour and a half's time the train would creep into Dublin, and he'd take a taxi. He'd spend a night in the Gresham Hotel, probably falling in with another priest, having a drink or two, maybe playing a game of bridge after his meal. That was his brother's way and always had been — an extravagant, easy kind of way, full of smiles and good humour. It was what had taken him to America and made him successful there. In order to raise money for the church that he and Father Steigmuller intended to build before 1980 he took parties of the well-to-do from San Francisco to Rome and Florence, to Chartres and Seville and the Holy Land. He was good at raising money, not just for the church but for the boys' home of which he was president, and for the Hospital of Our Saviour, and for St. Mary's Old People's Home on the west side of the city. But every July he flew back to Ireland, to the town in Co. Tipperary where his mother and brother and sister still lived. He stayed in the house above the shop which he might have inherited himself on the death of his father, which he'd rejected in favour of the religious life. Mrs. Daly was eighty now. In the shop she sat silently behind the counter, in a corner by the chicken-wire, wearing only clothes that were black. In the evenings she sat with Francis in the lace-curtained sitting-room, while the rest of the family occupied the kitchen. It was for her sake most of all that Father Paul made the journey every summer, considering it his duty.

Walking back to the town from the station, Francis was aware that he was missing his brother. Father Paul was fourteen years older than he and in childhood had often taken the place of their father, who had died when Francis was five. His brother had possessed an envied strength and knowledge; he'd been a hero, quite often worshipped, an example of success. In later life he had become an example of generosity as well: ten years ago he'd taken their mother to Rome, and their sister Kitty and her husband two years later; he'd paid the expenses when their sister Edna had gone to Canada; he'd assisted two nephews to make a start in America. In childhood Francis hadn't possessed his brother's healthy freckled face, just as in middle age he didn't have his ruddy complexion and his stoutness and his easiness with people. Francis was slight, his sandy hair receding, his face rather pale. His breathing was sometimes laboured because of wheeziness in the chest. In the ironmonger's shop he wore a brown cotton coat.

'Hullo, Mr. Daly,' a woman said to him in the main street of the town. 'Father Paul's gone off, has he?'

'Yes, he's gone again.'

'I'll pray for his journey so,' the woman promised, and Francis thanked her.

*

A year went by. In San Francisco another wing of the boys' home was completed, another target was reached in Father Paul's and Father Steigmuller's fund for the church they planned to have built by 1980. In the town in Co. Tipperary there were baptisms and burial services and First Communions. Old Loughlin, a farmer from Bansha, died in Flynn's grocery and bar, having gone there to celebrate a good price he'd got for a heifer. Clancy, from behind the counter in Doran's drapery, married Maureen Talbot; Mr. Nolan's plasterer married Miss Driscoll; Johneen Lynch married Seamus in the chip shop, under pressure from her family to do so. A local horse, from the stables on the Limerick road, was said to be an entry for the Fairyhouse Grand National, but it turned out not to be true. Every evening of that year Francis sat with his mother in the lace-curtained sitting-room above the shop. Every weekday she sat in her corner by the chicken-wire, watching while he counted out screws and weighed staples, or advised about yard brushes or tap-washers. Occasionally, on a Saturday, he visited the three Christian Brothers who lodged with Mrs. Shea and afterwards he'd tell his mother about how the authority was slipping these days from the nuns and the

Christian Brothers, and how Mrs. Shea's elderly maid, Agnes, couldn't see to cook the food any more. His mother would nod and hardly ever speak. When he told a joke, what young Hogan had said when he'd found a nail in his egg or how Agnes had put mint sauce into a jug with milk in it, she never laughed and looked at him in surprise when he laughed himself. But Dr. Grady said it was best to keep her cheered up.

All during that year Francis talked to her about his forthcoming visit to the Holy Land, endeavouring to make her understand that for a fortnight next spring he would be away from the house and the shop. He'd been away before for odd days, but that was when she'd been younger. He used to visit an aunt in Tralee, but three years ago the aunt had died and he hadn't left the town since.

Francis and his mother had always been close. Before his birth two daughters had died in infancy, and his very survival had often struck Mrs. Daly as a gift. He had always been her favourite, the one among her children whom she often considered least able to stand on his own two feet. It was just like Paul to have gone blustering off to San Francisco instead of remaining in Co. Tipperary. It was just like Kitty to have married a useless man. 'There's not a girl in the town who'd touch him,' she'd said to her daughter at the time, but Kitty had been headstrong and adamant, and there was Myles now, doing nothing whatsoever except cleaning other people's windows for a pittance and placing bets in Donovan's the turf accountant's. It was the shop and the arrangement Kitty had with Francis and her mother that kept her and the children going, three of whom had already left the town, which in Mrs. Daly's opinion they mightn't have done if they'd had a better type of father. She often wondered what the two babies who'd died might have grown up into, and imagined they might have been like Francis, about whom she'd never had a moment's worry. Not in a million years would he give you the feeling that he was too big for his boots, like Paul sometimes did with his lavishness and his big talk of

74

America. He wasn't silly like Kitty, or so sinful you couldn't forgive him, like you couldn't forgive Edna, even though she was dead and buried in Toronto.

Francis understood how his mother felt about the family. She'd had a hard life, left a widow early on, trying to do the best she could for everyone. In turn he did his best to compensate for the struggles and disappointments she'd suffered, cheering her in the evenings while Kitty and Myles and the youngest of their children watched the television in the kitchen. His mother had ignored the existence of Myles for ten years, ever since the day he'd taken money out of the till to pick up the odds on Gusty Spirit at Phoenix Park. And although Francis got on well enough with Myles he quite understood that there should be a long aftermath to that day. There'd been a terrible row in the kitchen, Kitty screaming at Myles and Myles telling lies and Francis trying to keep them calm, saying they'd give the old woman a heart attack.

She didn't like upsets of any kind, so all during the year before he was to visit the Holy Land Francis read the New Testament to her in order to prepare her. He talked to her about Bethlehem and Nazareth and the miracle of the loaves and fishes and all the other miracles. She kept nodding, but he often wondered if she didn't assume he was just casually referring to episodes in the Bible. As a child he had listened to such talk himself, with awe and fascination, imagining the walking on the water and the temptation in the wilderness. He had imagined the Cross carried to Calvary, and the rock rolled back from the tomb and the rising from the dead on the third day. That he was now to walk in such places seemed extraordinary to him, and he wished his mother was younger so that she could appreciate his good fortune and share it with him when she received the postcards he intended, every day, to send her. But her eyes seemed always to tell him that he was making a mistake, that somehow he was making a fool of himself by doing such a showy thing as going to the Holy Land. *I have the entire itinerary mapped out,* his brother wrote from

San Francisco. *There's nothing we'll miss.*

*

It was the first time Francis had been in an aeroplane. He flew by Aer Lingus from Dublin to London and then changed to an El AI flight to Tel Aviv. He was nervous and he found it exhausting. All the time he seemed to be eating, and it was strange being among so many people he didn't know. 'You will taste honey such as never before,' an Israeli businessman in the seat next to his assured him. 'And Galilean figs. Make certain to taste Galilean figs.' Make certain too, the businessman went on, to experience Jerusalem by night and in the early dawn. He urged Francis to see places he had never heard of, the Yad Va-Shem, the treasures of the Shrine of the Book. He urged him to honour the martyrs of Masada and to learn a few words of Hebrew as a token of respect. He told him of a shop where he could buy mementoes and warned him against Arab street traders.

'The hard man, how are you?' Father Paul said at Tel Aviv airport, having flown in from San Francisco the day before. Father Paul had had a drink or two and he suggested another when they arrived at the Plaza Hotel in Jerusalem. It was half-past nine in the evening. 'A quick little night cap,' Father Paul insisted, 'and then hop into bed with you, Francis.' They sat in an enormous open lounge with low, round tables and square modern armchairs. Father Paul said it was the bar.

They had said what had to be said in the car from Tel Aviv to Jerusalem. Father Paul had asked about their mother, and Kitty and Myles. He'd asked about other people in the town, old Canon Mahon and Sergeant Malone. He and Father Steigmuller had had a great year of it, he reported: as well as everything else, the boys' home had turned out two tip-top footballers. 'We'll start on a tour at half-nine in the morning,' he said. 'I'll be sitting having breakfast at eight.'

Francis went to bed and Father Paul ordered another whiskey, with ice. To his great disappointment there was no Irish whiskey in the hotel so he'd had to content himself with Haig. He fell into conversation with an American couple, making them promise that if they were ever in Ireland they wouldn't miss out Co. Tipperary. At eleven o'clock the barman said he was wanted at the reception desk and when Father Paul went upstairs and announced himself he was given a message in an envelope. It was a telegram that had come, the girl said in poor English. Then she shook her head, saying it was a telex. He opened the envelope and learnt that Mrs. Daly had died.

*

Francis fell asleep immediately and dreamed that he was a boy again, out fishing with a friend whom he couldn't now identify.

On the telephone Father Paul ordered whiskey and ice to be brought to his room. Before drinking it he took his jacket off and knelt by his bed to pray for his mother's salvation. When he'd completed the prayers he walked slowly up and down the length of the room, occasionally sipping at his whiskey. He argued with himself and finally arrived at a decision.

*

For breakfast they had scrambled eggs that looked like yellow ice-cream, and orange juice that was delicious. Francis wondered about bacon, but Father Paul explained that bacon was not readily available in Israel.

'Did you sleep all right?' Father Paul enquired. 'Did you have the jet-lag?'

'Jet-lag?'

'A tiredness you get after jet flights. It'd knock you out for days.'

'Ah, I slept great, Paul.'

'Good man.'

They lingered over breakfast. Father Paul reported a little more of what had happened in his parish during the year, in particular about the two young footballers from the boys' home. Francis told about the decline in the cooking at Mrs. Shea's boarding-house, as related to him by the three Christian Brothers. 'I have a car laid on,' Father Paul said, and twenty minutes later they walked out into the Jerusalem sunshine.

The hired car stopped on the way to the walls of the old city. It drew into a lay-by at Father Paul's request and the two men got out and looked across a wide valley dotted with houses and olive trees. A road curled along the distant slope opposite. 'The Mount of Olives,' Father Paul said. 'And that's the road to Jericho.' He pointed more particularly. 'You see that group of eight big olives? Just off the road, where the church is?'

Francis thought he did, but was not sure. There were so many olive trees, and more than one church. He glanced at his brother's pointing finger and followed its direction with his glance.

'The Garden of Gethsemane,' Father Paul said.

Francis did not say anything. He continued to gaze at the distant church, with the clump of olive trees beside it. Wild flowers were profuse on the slopes of the valley, smears of orange and blue on land that looked poor. Two Arab women herded goats.

'Could we see it closer?' he asked, and his brother said that definitely they would. They returned to the waiting car and Father Paul ordered it to the Gate of St. Stephen.

Tourists heavy with cameras thronged the Via Dolorosa. Brown, bare-foot children asked for alms. Stall-keepers pressed their different wares, cotton dresses, metal-ware, mementoes, sacred goods. 'Get out of the way,' Father Paul kept saying to them, genially laughing to show he wasn't being abrupt. Francis wanted to stand still and close his eyes, to visualise for a moment the carrying of the Cross. But the ceremony of the Stations, familiar to him for as long as he could remember, was unreal. Try as he would, Christ's journey refused to enter his imagination, and his own plain church seemed closer to the heart of the matter than the noisy lane he was now being jostled on. 'God damn it, of course it's genuine,' an angry American voice proclaimed, in reply to a shriller voice which insisted that cheating had taken place. The voices argued about a piece of wood, neat beneath plastic in a little box, a sample or not of the Cross that had been carried.

They arrived at the Church of Holy Sepulchre, and at the Chapel of the Nailing to the Cross, where they prayed. They passed through the Chapel of the Angel, to the tomb of Christ. Nobody spoke in the marble cell, but when they left the church Francis overheard a quiet man with spectacles saying it was unlikely that a body would have been buried within the walls of the city. They walked to Hezekiah's Pool and out of the old city at the Jaffa Gate, where their hired car was waiting for them. 'Are you peckish?' Father Paul asked, and although Francis said he wasn't they returned to the hotel.

Delay funeral till Monday was the telegram Father Paul had sent. There was an early flight on Sunday, in time for an afternoon one from London to Dublin. With luck there'd be a late train on Sunday evening and if there wasn't they'd have to fix a car. Today was Tuesday. It would give them four and a half days. *Funeral eleven Monday* the telegram at the reception desk now confirmed. 'Ah, isn't that great?' he said to himself, bundling the telegram up.

'Will we have a small one?' he suggested in the open area that was the bar. 'Or better still a big one.' He laughed. He was in good spirits in spite of the death that had taken place. He gestured at the barman, wagging his head and smiling jovially.

His pink face had reddened in the morning sun; there was specks of sweat on his forehead and his nose. 'Bethlehem this afternoon,' he laid down. 'Unless the jet-lag. . . ?'

'I haven't got the jet-lag.'

In the Nativity Boutique Francis bought for his mother a small metal dish with a fish on it. He had stood for a moment scarcely able to believe it, on the spot where the manger had been, in the Church of the Nativity. As in the Via Dolorosa, it had been difficult to rid the imagination of the surroundings that now were present, of the exotic Greek Orthodox trappings, the foreign-looking priests, the oriental smell. Gold, frankincense and myrrh, he'd kept thinking, for somehow the church seemed more the church of the Kings than of Joseph and Mary and their child. Afterwards they returned to Jerusalem, to the Tomb of the Virgin and the Garden of Gethsemane. 'It could have been anywhere,' he heard the quiet, bespectacled sceptic remarking in Gethsemane. 'They're only guessing.'

*

Father Paul rested in the late afternoon, lying down on his bed with his jacket off. He slept from half-past five until a quarter-past seven and awoke refreshed. He picked up the telephone and asked for whiskey and ice to be brought up and when it arrived he undressed and had a bath, relaxing in the warm water with the drink on a ledge in the tiled wall beside him. There would be time to take in Nazareth and Galilee. He was particularly keen that his brother should see Galilee because Galilee had atmosphere and was beautiful. There wasn't, in his own opinion, very much to Nazareth but it would be a pity to miss it all the same. It was at the Sea of Galilee that he intended to tell his brother of their mother's death.

We've had a great day, Francis wrote on a postcard that showed an aerial view of Jerusalem. *The Church of the Holy Sepulchre, where Our Lord's Tomb is, and Gethsemane and Bethlehem. Paul's in great form.* He addressed it to his mother, and then wrote other cards, to Kitty and Myles and to the three Christian Brothers in Mrs. Shea's, and to Canon Mahon. He gave thanks that he was privileged to be in Jerusalem. He read St. Mark and some of St. Matthew. He said his rosary.

'Will we chance the wine?' Father Paul said at dinner, not that wine was something he went in for, but a waiter had come up and put a large padded wine-list into his hand.

'Ah, no, no,' Francis protested. But already Father Paul was running his eye down the listed bottles.

'Have you local wine?' he enquired of the waiter. 'A nice red one?'

The waiter nodded and hurried away, and Francis hoped he wouldn't get drunk, the red wine on top of the whiskey he'd had in the bar before the meal. He'd only had the one whiskey, not being much used to it, making it last through his brother's three.

'I heard some gurriers in the bar,' Father Paul said, 'making a great song and dance about the local red wine.'

Wine made Francis think of the Holy Communion, but he didn't say so. He said the soup was delicious, and he drew his brother's attention to the custom there was in the hotel of a porter ringing a bell and walking about with a person's name chalked on a little blackboard on the end of a rod.

'It's a way of paging you,' Father Paul explained. 'Isn't it nicer than bellowing out some fellow's name?' He smiled his easy smile, his eyes beginning to water as a result of the few drinks he'd had. He was beginning to feel the strain: he kept thinking of their mother lying there, of what she'd say if she knew what he'd done, how she'd savagely upbraid him for keeping the fact from Francis. Out of duty and humanity he had returned each year to see her because, after all, you only had the one mother. But he had never cared for her.

Francis went for a walk after dinner. There were young soldiers with what seemed to be toy guns on the streets, but he knew the guns were real. In the shop windows there were television sets for sale, and furniture and clothes, just like anywhere else. There were advertisements for some film or other, two writhing women without a stitch on them, the kind of thing you wouldn't see in Co. Tipperary. 'You want something, sir?' a girl said, smiling at him with broken front teeth. The siren of a police car or an ambulance shrilled urgently near by. He shook his head at the girl. 'No, I don't want anything,' he said, and then realised what she had meant. She was small and very dark, no more than a child. He hurried on, praying for her.

When he returned to the hotel he found his brother in the lounge with other people, two men and two women. Father Paul was ordering a round of drinks and called out to the barman to bring another whiskey. 'Ah, no, no,' Francis protested, anxious to go to his room and to think about the day, to read the New Testament and perhaps to write a few more postcards. Music was playing, coming from speakers that could not be seen.

'My brother Francis,' Father Paul said to the people he was with, and the people all gave their names, adding that they came from New York. 'I was telling them about Tipp,' Father Paul said to his brother, offering his packet of cigarettes around.

'You like Jerusalem, Francis?' one of the American women asked him, and he replied that he hadn't been able to take it in yet. Then, feeling that that didn't sound enthusiastic enough, he added that being there was the experience of a lifetime.

Father Paul went on talking about Co. Tipperary and then spoke of his parish in San Francisco, the boys' home and the two promising footballers, the plans for the new church. The Americans listened and in a moment the conversation drifted on the subject of their travels in England, their visit to Istanbul and Athens, an argument they'd had with the Customs at Tel Aviv. 'Well, I'm for the hay-pile,' one of the men announced eventually, standing up.

The others stood up too and so did Francis. Father Paul remained where he was, gesturing again in the direction of the barman. 'Sit down for a night-cap,' he urged his brother.

'Ah, no, no —' Francis began.

'Bring us two more of those,' the priest ordered with a sudden abruptness, and the barman hurried away. 'Listen,' said Father Paul. 'I've something to tell you.'

After dinner, while Francis had been out on his walk, before he'd dropped into conversation with the Americans, Father Paul had said to himself that he couldn't stand the strain. It was the old woman stretched out above the hardware shop, as stiff as a board already, with the little lights burning in her room: he kept seeing all that, as if she wanted him to, as if she was trying to haunt him. Nice as the idea was, he didn't think he could continue to withhold the truth until they got up to Galilee.

Francis didn't want to drink any more. He hadn't wanted the whisky his brother had ordered him earlier, nor the one the Americans had ordered for him. He didn't want the one that the barman now brought. He thought he'd just leave it there, hoping his brother wouldn't see it. He lifted the glass to his lips, but he managed not to drink any.

'A bad thing has happened,' Father Paul said.

'Bad? How d'you mean, Paul?'

'Are you ready for it?' He paused. Then he said, 'She died.'

Francis didn't know what he was talking about. He didn't know who was meant to be dead, or why his brother was behaving in an odd manner. He didn't like to think it but he had to: his brother wasn't fully sober.

'Our mother died,' Father Paul said. 'I'm after getting a telegram.'

The huge area that was the bar of the Plaza Hotel, the endless tables and people sitting at them, the swiftly moving waiters and barmen, seemed suddenly a dream. Francis had a feeling that he was not where he appeared to be, that he wasn't sitting with his brother, who was wiping his lips with a handkerchief. For a moment he appeared in his confusion to be struggling his way up the Via Dolorosa again and then that he was in the Nativity Boutique.

'Take it easy, boy,' his brother was saying. 'Take a mouthful of whisky.'

Francis didn't obey that injunction. He asked his brother to repeat what he had said, and Father Paul repeated that their mother had died.

Francis closed his eyes and tried as well to shut away the sounds around them. He prayed for the salvation of his mother's soul. 'Blessed Virgin, intercede,' his own voice said in his mind. 'Dear Mary, let her few small sins be forgiven.'

Having rid himself of his secret, Father Paul felt instant relief. With the best of intentions, it had been a foolish idea to think he could maintain the secret until they arrived in a place that was perhaps the most suitable in the world to hear of the death of a person who'd been close to you. He took a gulp of his whisky and wiped his mouth with his handkerchief again. He watched his brother, waiting for his eyes to open.

'When did it happen?' Francis asked eventually.

'Yesterday.'

'And the telegram only came —'

'It came last night, Francis. I wanted to save you the pain.'

'Save me? How could you save me? I sent her a postcard, Paul.'

'Listen to me, Francis —'

'How could you save me the pain?'

'I wanted to tell you when we got up to Galilee.'

Again Francis felt he was caught in the middle of a dream. He couldn't understand his brother: he couldn't understand what he meant by saying a telegram had come last night, why at a moment like this he was talking about Galilee. He didn't know why he was sitting in this noisy place when he should be back in Ireland.

'I fixed the funeral for Monday,' Father Paul said.

Francis nodded, not grasping the significance of this arrangement. 'We'll be back there this time tomorrow,' he said.

'No need for that, Francis. Sunday morning's time enough.'

'But she's dead —'

'We'll be there in time for the funeral.'

'We can't stay here if she's dead.'

It was this, Father Paul realised, he'd been afraid of when he'd argued with himself and made his plan. If he'd have knocked on Francis's door the night before Francis would have wanted to return immediately without seeing a single stone of the land he had come so far to be moved by.

'We could go straight up to Galilee in the morning,' Father Paul said quietly. 'You'll find comfort in Galilee, Francis.'

But Francis shook his head. 'I want to be with her,' he said.

Father Paul lit another cigarette. He nodded at a hovering waiter, indicating his need of another drink. He said to himself that he must keep his cool, an expression he was fond of.

'Take it easy, Francis,' he said.

'Is there a plane out in the morning? Can we make arrangements now?' He looked about him as if for a member of the hotel staff who might be helpful.

'No good'll be done by tearing off home, Francis. What's wrong with Sunday?'

'I want to be with her.'

Anger swelled within Father Paul. If he began to argue his words would become slurred: he knew that from experience. He must keep his cool and speak slowly and clearly, making a few simple points. It was typical of her, he thought, to die inconveniently.

'You've come all this way,' he said as slowly as he could without sounding peculiar. 'Why cut it any shorter than we need? We'll be losing a week anyway. She wouldn't want us to go back.'

'I think she would.'

He was right in that. Her possessiveness in her lifetime

would have reached out across a dozen continents for Francis. She'd known what she was doing by dying when she had.

'I shouldn't have come,' Francis said. 'She didn't want me to come.'

'You're thirty-seven years of age, Francis.'

'I did wrong to come.'

'You did no such thing.'

The time he'd taken her to Rome she'd been difficult for the whole week, complaining about the food, saying everywhere was dirty. Whenever he'd spent anything she'd disapproved. All his life, Father Paul felt, he'd done his best for her. He had told her before anyone else when he'd decided to enter the priesthood, certain that she'd be pleased. 'I thought you'd take over the shop,' she'd said instead.

'What difference could it make to wait, Francis?'

'There's nothing to wait for.'

As long as he lived, Francis knew he would never forgive himself. As long as he lived, he would say to himself that he hadn't been able to wait a few years, until she'd passed quietly on. He might even have been in the room with her when it happened.

'It was a terrible thing not to tell me,' he said, 'I sat down and wrote her a postcard, Paul. I bought her a dish.'

'So you said.'

'You're drinking too much of that whiskey.'

'Now, Francis, don't be silly.'

'You're half drunk and she's lying there.'

'She can't be brought back no matter what we do.'

'She never hurt anyone,' Francis said.

Father Paul didn't deny that, although it wasn't true. She had hurt their Sister Kitty, constantly reproaching her for marrying the man she had, long after Kitty was aware she'd made a mistake. She'd driven Edna to Canada after Edna, still unmarried, had had a miscarriage that only the family knew about. She had made a shadow out of Francis although Francis didn't know it. Failing to hold on to her other children, she had grasped her last-born to her, as if she had borne him to destroy him.

'It'll be you'll say a mass for her?' Francis said.

'Yes, of course it will.'

'You should have told me.'

Francis realised why, all day, he'd been disappointed. From the moment when the hired car had pulled into the lay-by and his brother had pointed across the valley at the Garden of Gethsemane he'd been disappointed and had not admitted it. He'd been disappointed in the Via Dolorosa and in the Church of the Holy Sepulchre and in Bethlehem. He remembered the bespectacled man who'd kept saying that you couldn't be sure about anything. All the people with cameras made it impossible to think, all the jostling and pushing was distracting. When he'd said there'd been too much to take in he'd meant something different.

'Her death got in the way,' he said.

'What d'you mean, Francis?'

'It didn't feel like Jerusalem, it didn't feel like Bethlehem.'

'But it is, Francis, it is.'

'There are soldiers with guns all over the place. And a girl came up to me on the street. There was that man with a bit of the Cross. There's you, drinking and smoking in this place —'

'Now, listen to me, Francis —'

'Nazareth would be a disappointment. And the Sea of Galilee. And the Church of the Loaves and Fishes.' His voice had risen. He lowered it again. 'I couldn't believe in the Stations this morning. I couldn't see it happening the way I do at home.'

'That's nothing to do with her death, Francis. You've got a bit of jet-lag, you'll settle yourself up in Galilee. There's an atmosphere in Galilee that nobody misses.'

'I'm not going near Galilee.' He struck the surface of the table, and Father Paul told him to contain himself. People turned their heads, aware that anger had erupted in the pale-faced man with the priest.

'Quieten up,' Father Paul commanded sharply, but Francis didn't.

'She knew I'd be better at home,' he shouted, his voice shrill and reedy. 'She knew I was making a fool of myself, a man out of a shop trying to be big —'

'Will you keep your voice down? Of course you're not making a fool of yourself.'

'Will you find out about planes tomorrow morning?'

Father Paul sat for a moment longer, not saying anything, hoping his brother would say he was sorry. Naturally it was a shock, naturally he'd be emotional and feel guilty, in a moment it would be better. But it wasn't, and Francis didn't say he was sorry. Instead he began to weep.

'Let's go up to your room,' Father Paul said, 'and I'll fix about the plane.'

Francis nodded but did not move. His sobbing ceased, and then he said: 'I'll always hate the Holy Land now.'

'No need for that, Francis.'

But Francis felt there was and he felt he would hate, as well, the brother he had admired for as long as he could remember. In the bar of the Plaza Hotel he felt mockery surfacing everywhere. His brother's deceit, and the endless whiskey in his brother's glass, and his casualness after a death, seemed like the scorning of a Church which honoured so steadfastly the mother of its founder. Vivid in his mind, his own mother's eyes reminded him that they'd told him he was making a mistake, and upbraided him for not heeding her. Of course there was mockery everywhere, in the splinter of wood beneath plastic, and in the soldiers with guns that were not toys, and the writhing nakedness in the Holy City. He'd become part of it himself, sending postcards to the dead. Not speaking again to his brother, he went to his room to pray.

*

'Eight a.m., sir,' the girl at the reception desk said, and

Father Paul asked that arrangements should be made to book two seats on the plane, explaining that it was an emergency, that a death had occurred. 'It will be all right, sir,' the girl promised.

He went slowly downstairs to the bar. He sat in a corner and lit a cigarette and ordered two whiskies and ice, as if expecting a companion. He drank them both himself and ordered more. Francis would return to Co. Tipperary and after the funeral he would take up again the life she had ordained for him. In his brown cotton coat he would serve customers with nails and hinges and wire. He would regularly go to Mass and to Confession and to Men's Confraternity. He would sit alone in the lace-curtained sitting-room, lonely for the woman who had made him what he was, married forever to her memory.

Father Paul lit a fresh cigarette from the butt of the last one. He continued to order whiskey in two glasses. Already he could sense the hatred that Francis had earlier felt taking root in himself. He wondered if he would ever again return in July to Co. Tipperary, and imagined he would not.

At midnight he rose to make the journey to bed and found himself unsteady on his feet. People looked at him, thinking it disgraceful for a priest to be drunk in Jerusalem, with cigarette ash all over his clerical clothes.

The Time of Year

All that autumn, when they were both fourteen, they had talked about their Christmas swim. She'd had the idea: that on Christmas morning when everyone was still asleep they would meet by the boats on the strand at Ballyquin and afterwards quite casually say that they had been for a swim on Christmas Day. Whenever they met during that stormy October and November they wondered how fine the day might be, how cold or wet, and if the sea could possibly be frozen. They walked together on the cliffs, looking down at the breaking waves of the Atlantic, shivering in anticipation. They walked through the misty dusk of the town, lingering over the first signs of Christmas in the shops: coloured lights strung up, holly and Christmas trees and tinsel. They wondered if people guessed about them. They didn't want them to, they wanted it to be a secret. People would laugh because they were children. They were in love that autumn.

Six years later Valerie still remembered, poignantly, in November. Dublin, so different from Ballyquin, stirred up the past as autumn drifted into winter and winds bustled around the grey buildings of Trinity College, where she was now a student. The city's trees were bleakly bare, it seemed to Valerie; there was sadness, even, on the lawns of her hall of residence, scattered with finished leaves. In her small room, preparing herself one Friday evening for the Skullys' end-of-term party, she sensed quite easily the Christmas chill of the sea, the chilliness creeping slowly over her calves and knees. She paused with the memory, gazing at herself in the looking-glass attached to the inside of her cupboard door. She was a tall girl, standing now in a white silk petticoat, with a thin face and thin long fingers and an almost classical nose. Her black hair was as straight as a die, falling to her shoulders. She was pretty when she smiled and she did so at her reflection, endeavouring to overcome the melancholy that visited her at this time of year. She turned away and picked up a green corduroy dress which she had laid out on her bed. She was going to be late if she dawdled like this.

*

The parties given by Professor and Mrs. Skully were renowned neither for the entertainment they provided nor for their elegance. They were, unfortunately, difficult to avoid, the Professor being persistent in the face of repeated excuses — a persistence it was deemed unwise to strain.

Bidden for half-past seven, his History students came on bicycles, a few in Kilroy's Mini, Ruth Cusper on her motor-cycle, Bewley Joal on foot. Woodward, Whipp and Woolmer-Mills came cheerfully, being kindred spirits of the Professor's and in no way dismayed by the immediate prospect. Others were apprehensive or cross, trying not to let it show as smilingly they entered the Skullys' house in Rathgar.

'How very nice!' Mrs. Skully murmured in a familiar manner in the hall. 'How jolly good of you to come.'

The hall was not yet decorated for Christmas, but the Professor had found the remains of last year's crackers and had stuck half a dozen behind the heavily framed scenes of Hanover that had been established in the hall since the early days of the Skullys' marriage. The gaudy crêpe paper protruded above the pictures in splurges of green, red and yellow, and cheered up the hall to a small extent. The coloured scarves and overcoats of the History students, already accumulating on the hall-stand, did so more effectively.

In the Skullys' sitting-room the Professor's record-player, old and in some way special, was in its usual place:

on a mahogany table in front of the French windows, which were now obscured by brown curtains. Four identical rugs, their colour approximately matching that of the curtains, were precisely arranged on darker brown linoleum. Rexine-seated dining-chairs lined brownish walls.

The Professor's History students lent temporary character to this room, as their coats and scarves did to the hall. Kilroy was plump in a royal-blue suit. The O'Neill sisters' cluster of followers, jostling even now for promises of favours, wore carefully pressed denim or tweed. The O'Neill sisters themselves exuded a raffish, cocktail-time air. They were twins, from Lurgan, both of them blonde and both favouring an excess of eye-shadow, and lipstick that wetly gleamed, the same shade of pink as the trouser suits that nudgingly hugged the protuberances of their bodies. Not far from where they now held court, the rimless spectacles of Bewley Joal had a busy look in the room's harsh light; the complexion of Yvonne Smith was displayed to disadvantage. So was the troublesome fair hair of Honor Hitchcock, who was engaged to a student known as the Reverend because of his declared intention one day to claim the title. Cosily in a corner she linked her arm with his, both of them seeming middle-aged before their time, inmates already of a draughty rectory in Co. Cork or Clare. 'I'll be the first,' Ruth Cusper vowed, 'to visit you in your parish. Wherever it is.' Ruth Cusper was a statuesque English girl, not yet divested of her motor-cycling gear.

The colours worn by the girls, and the denim and tweed, and the royal blue of Kilroy contrasted sharply with the uncared-for garb of Woodward, Whipp and Woolmer-Mills, all of whom were expected to take Firsts. Stained and frayed, these three hung together without speaking, Woodward very tall, giving the impression of an etiolated newt, Whipp small, his glasses repaired with Sellotape, Woolmer-Mills for ever launching himself back and forth on the balls of his feet.

In a pocket of Kilroy's suit there was a miniature bottle of vodka, for only tea and what the Professor described as 'cup' were served in the course of the evening. Kilroy fingered it, smiling across the room at the Professor, endeavouring to give the impression that he was delighted to be present. He was a student who was fearful of academic failure, his terror being that he would not get a Third: he had set his sights on a Third, well aware that to have set them higher would not be wise. He brought his little bottles of vodka to the Professor's parties as an act of bravado, a gesture designed to display jauntiness, to show that he could take a chance. But the chances he took with his vodka were not great.

Bewley Joal, who would end up with a respectable Second, was laying down the law to Yvonne Smith, who would be grateful to end up with anything at all. Her natural urge to chatter was stifled, for no one could get a word in when the clanking voice of Bewley Joal was in full flow. 'Oh, it's far more than just a solution, dear girl,' he breezily pronounced, speaking of Moral Rearmament. Yvonne Smith nodded and agreed, trying to say that an aunt of hers thought most highly of Moral Rearmament, that she herself had always been meaning to look into it. But the voice of Bewley Joal cut all her sentences in half.

'I thought we'd start,' the Professor announced, having coughed and cleared his throat, 'with the *Pathétique*.' He fiddled with the record-player while everyone sat down, Ruth Cusper on the floor. He was a biggish man in a grey suit that faintly recalled the clothes of Woodward, Whipp and Woolmer-Mills. On a large head hair was still in plentiful supply even though the Professor was fifty-eight. The hair was grey also, bushing out around his head in a manner that suggested professorial vagueness rather than a gesture in the direction of current fashion. His wife, who stood by his side while he placed a record on the turntable, wore a magenta skirt and twin-set and a string of jade beads. In almost every way — including this lively choice of dress — she seemed naturally to complement her husband, to fill the gaps his personality couldn't be bothered with. Her nervous manner was the opposite of his confident one. He gave his parties out of duty, and having done so found it hard to take an interest in any students except those who had already proved themselves academically sound. Mrs. Skully preferred to strike a lighter note. Now and again she made efforts to entice a few of the girls to join her on Saturday evenings, offering the suggestion that they might listen together to Saturday Night Theatre and afterwards sit around and discuss it. Because the Professor saw no point in television there was none in the Skullys' house.

Tchaikovsky filled the sitting-room. The professor sat down and then Mrs. Skully did. The doorbell rang.

*

'Ah, of course,' Mrs. Skully said.

'Valerie Upcott,' Valerie said. 'Good evening, Mrs. Skully.'

'Come in, come in, dear. The *Pathétique's* just started.' She remarked in the hall on the green corduroy dress that was revealed when Valerie took off her coat. The green was of so dark a shade that it might almost have been black. It had large green buttons all down the front. 'Oh, how really nice!' Mrs. Skully said.

The crackers that decorated the scenes of Hanover looked sinister, Valerie thought: Christmas was on the way, soon there'd be the coloured lights and imitation snow. She smiled at Mrs. Skully. She wondered about saying that her magenta outfit was nice also, but decided against it. 'We'll slip in quietly,' Mrs. Skully said.

Valerie tried to forget the crackers as she entered the sitting-room and took her place on a chair, but in her mind the brash images remained. They did so while she acknowledged Kilroy's winking smile and while she glanced towards the Professor in case he chose to greet her. But the Professor, his head bent over clasped hands, did not look up.

Among the History students Valerie was an unknown quantity. During the two years they'd all known one another she'd established herself as a person who was particularly quiet. She had a private look even when she smiled, when the thin features of her face were startled out of tranquillity, as if an electric light had suddenly been turned on. Kilroy still tried to take her out, Ruth Cusper was pally. But Valerie's privacy, softened by her sudden smile, unfussily repelled these attentions.

For her part she was aware of the students' curiosity, and yet she could not have said to any one of them that a tragedy which had occurred was not properly in the past yet. She could not mention the tragedy to people who didn't know about it already. She couldn't tell it as a story because to her it didn't seem in the least like that. It was a fact you had to live with, half wanting to forget it, half feeling you could not. This time of year and the first faint signs of Christmas were enough to tease it brightly into life.

The second movement of the *Pathétique* came to an end, the Professor rose to turn the record over, the students murmured. Mrs. Skully slipped away, as she always did at this point, to attend to matters in the kitchen. While the Professor was bent over the record-player Kilroy waved his bottle of vodka about and then raised it to his lips. 'Hullo, Valerie,' Yvonne Smith whispered across the distance that separated them. She endeavoured to continue her communication by shaping words with her lips. Valerie smiled at her and at Ruth Cusper, who had turned her head when she'd heard Yvonne Smith's greeting. 'Hi,' Ruth Cusper said.

The music began again. The mouthing of Yvonne Smith continued for a moment and then ceased. Valerie didn't notice that, because in the room the students and the Professor were shadows of a kind, the music a distant piping. The swish of wind was in the room, and the shingle, cold on her bare feet; so were the two flat stones they'd placed on their clothes to keep them from blowing away.

White flecks in the air were snow, she said: Christmas snow, what everyone wanted. But he said the flecks were flecks of foam.

He took her hand, dragging her a bit because the shingle hurt the soles of her feet and slowed her down. He hurried on the sand, calling back to her, reminding her that it was her idea, laughing at her hesitation. He called out something else as he ran into the breakers, but she couldn't hear because of the roar of the sea. She stood in the icy shallows and when she heard him shouting again she imagined he was still mocking her. She didn't even know he was struggling, she wasn't in the least aware of his death. It was his not being there she noticed, the feeling of being alone on the strand at Ballyquin.

'Cup, Miss Upcott?' the Professor offered in the dining-room. Poised above a glass, a jug contained a yellowish liquid. She said she'd rather have tea.

There were egg sandwiches and cakes, plates of crisps, biscuits and Twiglets. Mrs. Skully poured tea, Ruth Cusper handed round the cups and saucers. The O'Neill sisters and their followers shared an obscene joke, which was a game that had grown up at the Skullys' parties: one student doing his best to make the others giggle too noisily. A point was gained if the Professor demanded to share the fun.

'Oh, but of course there isn't any argument,' Bewley Joal was insisting, still talking to Yvonne Smith about Moral Rearmament. Words had ceased to dribble from her lips. Instead she kept nodding her head. 'We live in times of decadence,' Bewley Joal pronounced.

Woodward, Whipp and Woolmer-Mills were still together, Woolmer-Mills launching himself endlessly on to the balls of his feet, Whipp sucking at his cheeks. No conversation was taking place among them: when the Professor finished going round with his jug of cup, talk of some kind would begin, probably about a mediaeval document Woodward had earlier mentioned. Or about a reference to *panni streit sine grano* which had puzzled

Woolmer-Mills.

'Soon be Christmas,' Honor Hitchcock remarked to Valerie.

'Yes, it will.'

'I love it. I love the way you can imagine everyone doing just the same things on Christmas Eve, tying up presents, running around with holly, listening to the carols. And Christmas Day: that same meal in millions of houses, and the same prayers. All over the world.'

'Yes, there's that.'

'Oh, I think it's marvellous.'

'Christmas?' Kilroy said, suddenly beside them. He laughed, the fat on his face shaking a bit. 'Much over-rated in my small view.' He glanced as he spoke at the Professor's profile, preparing himself in case the Professor should look in his direction. His expression changed, becoming solemn.

There were specks of dandruff, Valerie noticed, on the shoulders of the Professor's grey suit. She thought it odd that Mrs. Skully hadn't drawn his attention to them. She thought it odd that Kilroy was so determined about his Third. And that Yvonne Smith didn't just walk away from the clanking voice of Bewley Joal.

'Orange or coffee?' Ruth Cusper proferred two cakes that had been cut into slices. The fillings in Mrs. Skully's cakes were famous, made with Trex and castor sugar. The cakes themselves had a flat appearance, like large biscuits.

'I wouldn't touch any of that stuff,' Kilroy advised, jocular again. 'I was up all night after it last year.'

'Oh, nonsense!' Ruth Cusper placed a slice of orange cake on Valerie's plate, making a noise that indicated she found Kilroy's attempt at wit a failure. She passed on, and Kilroy without reason began to laugh.

Valerie looked at them, her eyes pausing on each face in the room. She was different from these people of her own age because of her autumn melancholy and the bitterness of Christmas. A solitude had been made for her, while they belonged to each other, separate yet part of a whole.

97

She thought about them, envying them their ordinary normality, the good fortune they accepted as their due. They trailed no horror, no ghosts or images that wouldn't go away: you could tell that by looking at them. Had she herself already been made peculiar by all of it, eccentric and strange and edgy? And would it never slip away, into the past where it belonged? Each year it was the same, no different from the year before, intent on hanging on to her. Each year she smiled and made an effort. She was brisk with it, she did her best. She told herself she had to live with it, agreeing with herself that of course she had to, as if wishing to be overheard. And yet to die so young, so pointlessly and so casually, seemed to be something you had to feel unhappy about. It dragged out tears from you; it made you hesitate again, standing in the icy water. Your idea it had been.

'Tea, you people?' Mrs. Skully offered.

'Awfully kind of you, Mrs. Skully,' Kilroy said. 'Splendid tea this is.'

'I should have thought you'd be keener on the Professor's cup, Mr. Kilroy.'

'No, I'm not a cup man, Mrs. Skully.'

Valerie wondered what it would be like to be Kilroy. She wondered about his private thoughts, even what he was thinking now as he said he wasn't a cup man. She imagined him in his bedroom, removing his royal-blue suit and meticulously placing it on a hanger, talking to himself about the party, wondering if he had done himself any damage in the Professor's eyes. She imagined him as a child, plump in bathing-trunks, building a sandcastle. She saw him in a kitchen, standing on a chair by an open cupboard, nibbling the corner of a Chivers' jelly.

She saw Ruth Cusper too, bossy at a children's party, friendlily bossy, towering over other children. She made them play a game and wasn't disappointed when they didn't like it. You couldn't hurt Ruth Cusper; she'd grown an extra skin beneath her motor-cycling gear. At night, she often said, she fell asleep as soon as her head touched the pillow.

You couldn't hurt Bewley Joal, either: a grasping child, Valerie saw him as, quite quiet, watchful and charmless. Once he'd been hurt, she speculated: another child had told him that no one enjoyed playing with him, and he'd resolved from that moment not to care about stuff like that, to push his way through other people's opinion of him, not wishing to know it.

As children, the O'Neill sisters teased; their faithful tormentors pulled their hair. Woodward, Whipp and Woolmer-Mills read the *Children's Encyclopaedia*. Honor Hitchcock and the Reverend played mummies and daddies. 'Oh, listen to that chatterbox!' Yvonne Smith's father dotingly cried, affection that Yvonne Smith had missed ever since.

In the room the clanking of Bewley Joal punctuated the giggling in the corner where the O'Neill sisters were. More tea was poured and more of the Professor's cup, more cake was handed round. 'Ah, yes,' the Professor began. '*Panni streit sine grano.*' Woodward, Whipp and Woolmer-Mills bent their heads to listen.

The Professor, while waiting on his upstairs landing for Woolmer-Mills to use the lavatory, spoke of the tomatoes he grew. Similarly delayed downstairs, Mrs. Skully suggested to the O'Neill sisters that they might like, one Saturday night next term, to listen to Saturday Night Theatre with her. It was something she enjoyed, she said, especially the discussion afterwards. 'Or you, Miss Upcott,' she said. 'You've never been to one of my evenings either.'

Valerie smiled politely, moving with Mrs. Skully towards the sitting-room, where Tchaikovsky once more resounded powerfully. Again she examined the arrayed faces. Some eyes were closed in sleep, others were weary beneath a weight of tedium. Woodward's newt-like countenance had not altered, nor had Kilroy's fear dissipated. Frustration still tugged at Yvonne Smith. Nothing much was happening in the face of Mrs. Skully.

Valerie continued to regard Mrs. Skully's face and suddenly she found herself shivering. How could that mouth open and close, issuing invitations without knowing they were the subject of derision? How could this woman, in her late middle age, officiate at student parties in magenta and jade, or bake inedible cakes without knowing it? How could she daily permit herself to be taken for granted by a man who cared only for students with academic success behind them? How could she have married his pomposity in the first place? There was something wrong with Mrs. Skully, there was something missing, as if some part of her had never come to life. The more Valerie examined her the more extraordinary Mrs. Skully seemed, and then it seemed extraordinary that the Professor should be unaware that no one liked his parties. It was as if some part of him hadn't come to life either, as if they lived together in the dead wood of a relationship, together in this house because it was convenient.

She wondered if the other students had ever thought that, or if they'd be bothered to survey in any way whatsoever the Professor and his wife. She wondered if they saw a reflection of the Skullys' marriage in the brownness of the room they all sat in or in the crunchy fillings of Mrs. Skully's cakes, or in the Rexine-seated dining-chairs that were not comfortable. You couldn't blame them for not wanting to think about the Skullys' marriage: what good could come of it? The other students were busy and more organised than she. They had aims in life. They had futures she could sense, as she had sensed their pasts. Honor Hitchcock and the Reverend would settle down as right as rain in a provincial rectory, the followers of the O'Neill sisters would enter various business worlds. Woodward, Whipp and Woolmer-Mills would be the same as the Professor, dandruff on the shoulders of three grey suits. Bewley Joal would rise to heights, Kilroy would not. Ruth Cusper would run a hall of residence in Lurgan, the O'Neill sisters would give two husbands hell. Yvonne Smith would live in hopes.

The music of Tchaikovsky gushed over these reflections, as if to soften some harshness in them. But to Valerie there was no harshness in her contemplation of these people's lives, only fact and a lacing of speculation. The Skullys would go on ageing and he might never turn to his wife and say he was sorry. The O'Neill sisters would lose their beauty and Bewley Joal his vigour. One day Woolmer-Mills would find that he could no longer launch himself on to the balls of his feet. Kilroy would enter a home for the senile. Death would shatter the cotton-wool cosiness of Honor Hitchcock and the Reverend.

She wondered what would happen if she revealed what she had thought, if she told them that in order to keep her melancholy in control she had played about with their lives, seeing them in childhood, visiting them with old age and death. Which of them would seek to stop her while she cited the arrogance of the Professor and the pusillanimity of his wife? She heard her own voice echoing in a silence, telling them finally, in explanation, of the tragedy in her own life.

*

'Please all have a jolly Christmas,' Mrs. Skully urged in the hall as scarves and coats were lifted from the hall-stand. 'Please now.'

'We shall endeavour so,' Kilroy promised, and the others made similar remarks, wishing Mrs. Skully a happy Christmas herself, thanking her and the Professor for the party, Kilroy adding that it had been most enjoyable. There'd be another, the Professor promised, in May.

There was the roar of Ruth Cusper's motor-cycle, and the overloading of Kilroy's Mini, and the striding into the night of Bewley Joal, and others making off on bicycles. Valerie walked with Yvonne Smith through the suburban roads. 'I quite like Joal,' Yvonne Smith confided, releasing the first burst of her pent-up chatter. 'He's all right, isn't he? Quite nice, really, quite clever. I mean if you care for a clever kind of person. I mean, I wouldn't mind going out with him if he asked me.'

Valerie agreed that Bewley Joal was all right if you cared for that kind of person. It was pleasant in the cold night air. It was good that the party was over.

Yvonne Smith said good-night, still chattering about Bewley Joal as she turned into the house where her lodgings were. Valerie walked on alone, a thin shadow in the gloom. Compulsively now, she thought about the party, seeing again the face of Mrs. Skully and the Professor's face and the faces of the others. They formed, like a backdrop in her mind, an assembly as vivid as the tragedy that more grimly visited it. They seemed like the other side of the tragedy, as if she had for the first time managed to peer round a corner. The feeling bewildered her. It was odd to be left with it after the Skullys' end-of-term party.

In the garden of the hall of residence the fallen leaves were sodden beneath her feet as she crossed a lawn to shorten her journey. The bewilderment she felt lifted a little. She had been wrong to imagine she envied other people their normality and good fortune. She was as she wished to be. She paused in faint moonlight, repeating that to herself and then repeating it again. She did not quite add that the tragedy had made her what she was, that without it she would not possess her reflective introspection, or be sensitive to more than just the time of year. But the thought hovered with her as she moved towards the lights of the house, offering what appeared to be a hint of comfort.

Attracta

Attracta read about Penelope Vade in a newspaper, an item that upset her. It caused her to wonder if all her life as a teacher she'd been saying the wrong things to the children in her care. It saddened her when she thought about the faces that had passed through her schoolroom, ever since 1937. She began to feel she should have told them about herself.

She taught in a single schoolroom that hadn't altered much since the days when she'd been a pupil in it herself. There were portraits of England's kings and queens around the walls, painted by some teacher in the past. There were other pictures, added at some later date, of Irish heroes: Niall of the Nine Hostages, Lord Edward Fitzgerald, Wolfe Tone and Grattan. Maps of Europe and of Ireland and of England, Wales and Scotland hung side by side. A new blackboard attached to the wall, had ten years ago replaced the old pedestal one. The globe had always been there in Attracta's time, but since it did not designate political boundaries it wasn't much out of date. The twenty-five wooden desks more urgently needed to be replaced.

In the schoolroom Attracta taught the sixteen Protestant children of the town. The numbers had been sometimes greater in the past, and often fewer; sixteen was an average, a number she found easy to manage when divided into the four classes that the different ages demanded. The room was large, the desks arranged in groups, discipline had never been a problem. The country children brought sandwiches for lunch, the children of the town went home at midday. Attracta went home herself, to the house in North Street which she'd inherited from her Aunt Emmeline and where now she lived alone. She possessed an old blue Morris Minor but she did not often drive it to and from her schoolroom, preferring to make the journey on foot in order to get fresh air and exercise. She was a familiar figure, the Protestant teacher with her basket of groceries or exercise-books. She had never married, though twice she'd been proposed to: by an exchange clerk in the Provincial Bank and by an English visitor to the area who'd once spent the summer in the area with his parents. All that was a long time ago now, for Attracta was sixty-one. Her predecessor in the schoolroom, Mr. Ayrie, hadn't retired until he was over seventy. She had always assumed she'd emulate him in that.

Looking back on it, Attracta didn't regret that she had not married. She hadn't much cared for either of the men who'd proposed to her and she didn't mind being alone at sixty-one in her house in North Street. She regularly went to church, she had friends among the people who had been her pupils in the past. Now and again in the holidays she drove her Morris Minor to Cork for a day's shopping and possibly a visit to the Savoy or the Pavilion, although the films they offered were not as good as they'd been in the past. Being on her own was something she'd always known, having been both an only child and an orphan. There'd been tragedy in her life but she considered that she had not suffered. People had been good to her.

English Girl's Suicide in Belfast the headline about Penelope Vade said, and below it there was a photograph, a girl with a slightly crooked smile and freckled cheeks. There was a photograph of her husband in army uniform, taken a few weeks before his death, and of the house in Belfast in which she had later rented a flat. *From the marks of blood on carpets and rugs*, the item said, *it is deduced that Mrs. Vade dragged herself across the floors of two rooms. She appears repeatedly to have fainted before she reached a bottle of aspirins in a kitchen cupboard.* She had been twenty-three at the time of her death.

It was Penelope Vade's desire to make some kind of gesture, a gesture of courage and perhaps anger, that had caused her to leave her parents' home in Haslemere and to go to Belfast. Her husband, an army officer, had been murdered in Belfast; he'd been decapitated as well. His head, wrapped in cotton-wool to absorb the ooze of blood, secured within a plastic bag and packed in a biscuit-tin, had been posted to Penelope Vade. Layer by layer the parcel had been opened by her in Haslemere. She hadn't known that he was dead before his dead eyes stared into hers.

Her gesture was her mourning of him. She went to Belfast to join the Women's Peace Movement, to make the point that somehow neither he nor she had been defeated. But her gesture, publicly reported, had incensed the men who'd gone to the trouble of killing him. One after another, seven of them had committed acts of rape on her. It was after that that she had killed herself.

A fortnight after Attracta had first read the newspaper item it still upset her. It haunted her, and she knew why it did, though only imprecisely. Alone at night, almost catching her unawares, scenes from the tragedy established themselves in her mind: the opening of the biscuit-box, the smell of death, the eyes, blood turning brown. As if at a macabre slide-show, the scene would change: before people had wondered about her whereabouts Penelope Vade had been dead for four days; mice had left droppings on her body.

One afternoon, in order to think the matter over in peace and quiet, Attracta drove her Morris Minor to the sea at Cedarstrand, eight miles from the town. She clambered from the strand up to the headland and paused there, gazing down into the bay, at the solitary island it held. No one had ever lived on the island because its smallness would have made a self-supporting existence impossible. When she'd been growing up she'd often wondered what it would be like to live alone on the rocky fastness, in a wooden hut or a cottage built of stones. Not very agreeable, she'd thought, for she'd always been sociable. She thought it again as she turned abruptly from the sea and followed a path inland through wiry purple heather.

Two fishermen, approaching her on the path, recognised her as the Protestant teacher from the town eight miles away and stood aside for her to pass. She was thinking that nothing she might ever have said in her schoolroom could possibly have prevented the death of a girl in a city two hundred miles away. Yet in a way it seemed ridiculous that for so long she had been relating the details of Cromwell's desecration and the laws of Pythagoras, when she should have been talking about Mr. Devereux and Geraldine Carey. And it was Mr. Purce she should have recalled instead of the Battle of the Boyne.

The fishermen spoke to her as she passed them by but she didn't reply. It surprised them that she didn't, for they hadn't heard that the Protestant teacher had recently become deaf or odd. Just old, they supposed as they watched her progressing slowly: an upright figure, spare and seeming fragile, a certain stiffness in her movement.

*

What made Attracta feel close to the girl in the newspaper item was the tragedy of her own life: the death of her mother and her father when she was three. Her parents had gone away, she had been told, and at first she had wept miserably and would not be comforted. But as days passed into weeks, and weeks into months, this unhappiness gradually left her. She ceased to ask about her parents and became used to living in her Aunt Emmeline's house in North Street. In time she no longer remembered the morning she'd woken up in this house in a bed that was strange to her; nor could she recollect her parents' faces. She grew up assuming they were no longer alive and when once she voiced this assumption her aunt did not contradict it. It wasn't until later in her childhood, when she was eleven, that she learnt the details of the tragedy from Mr. Purce, a small man in a hard black hat, who was often to be seen on the streets of the town. He was one of the people she noticed in her childhood, like the elderly beggar-woman called Limerick Nancy and the wild-looking builder's labourer who could walk a hundred miles without stopping, who never wore a jersey or a coat over his open shirt even on the coldest winter days. There were other people too: priests going for a walk in pairs, out along the road that led to the golf-course and to Cedarstrand by the longer route. Strolling through the afternoon sunshine there were nuns in pairs also, and there was Redmond the solicitor hurrying about with his business papers, and Father Quinn on his bicycle. At night there were the red-fleshed country bachelors tipsily smiling through cigarette smoke, lips glistening in the street-light outside Keogh's public house. At all times of day, at all the town's corners, the children of the poor waited for nothing in particular.

The town was everything in Attracta's childhood, and only some of it had changed in the fifty years that had passed. Without nostalgia she remembered now the horses and carts with milk churns for the creamery, slowly advancing on narrow streets between colour-washed houses. On fair days the pavements had been slithery with dung, and on fair days they still were. Farmers stood by their animals, their shirts clean for the occasion, a stud at their throats, without collar or tie. Dogs slouched in a manner that was characteristic of the dogs of the town; there was a smell of stout and sawdust. In her childhood there had been O'Mara's Picture House, dour grey cement encasing the dreamland of Fred Astaire and Ginger Rogers. Built with pride in 1929, O'Mara's was a ruin now.

Within the world of the town there had been, for Attracta, a smaller, Protestant world. Behind green railings there was Mr. Ayrie's Protestant schoolroom. There was the Church of Ireland church, with its dusty flags of another age, and Archdeacon Flower's prayers for the English royal family. There were the Sunday-school classes of Mr. and Mrs. Bell, and the patience of her aunt, which seemed like a Protestant thing also — the Protestant duty of a woman who had never expected to find herself looking after a child. There was Mr. Devereux, a Protestant who never went to church.

No one in the town, not even her aunt, was kinder to Attracta than Mr. Devereux. On her birthday he came himself to the house in North Street with a present carefully wrapped, a doll's house once, so big he'd had to ask the man next door to help him out of the dickey of his motor-car with it. At Christmas he had a Christmas tree in his house, and other children in the town, her friends from school, were invited to a party. Every Saturday she spent the afternoon with him, eating his housekeeper's delicious orange cake for tea and sticking stamps into the album he'd given her, listening to his gramophone in the room he called his office. He loved getting a huge fire going in his office, banking up the coals so that they'd glow and redden her cheeks. In summer he sat in his back garden with her, sometimes reading *The Coral Island* aloud. He made her run away to the raspberry canes and come back with a punnet of fruit which they'd have at suppertime. He was different from her aunt and from Mr. Ayrie and Archdeacon Flower. He smelt of the tobacco he smoked in his pipe. He wore tweed suits and a striped shirt with a white celluloid collar, and patterned brown shoes which Attracta greatly admired. His tie matched the tweed of his suit, a gold watch dangled from the lapel of his jacket into his top pocket. He was by trade a grain merchant.

His house was quiet and always a little mysterious. The drawing-room, full of looming furniture, was dark in the daytime. Behind layers of curtains that hung to the ground blue blinds obscured the greater part of the light: sunshine would damage the furniture, Mr. Devereux's housekeeper used to say. On a summer's afternoon this woman would light a paraffin lamp so that she could polish the mahogany surfaces of the tables and the grand piano. Her name was Geraldine Carey: she added to the house's mystery.

Mr. Devereux's smile was slow. There was a laziness about it, both in its leisurely arrival and the way it lingered. His eyes had a weary look, quite out of keeping with all the efforts he made to promote his friendship with Attracta and her aunt. Yet the efforts seemed natural to Attracta, as were the efforts of Geraldine Carey, who was the quietest person Attracta had ever met. She spoke in a voice that it was often hard to hear. Her hair was as black as coal, drawn back from her face and arranged in a coiled bun at the back of her head. Her eyes were startlingly alive, seeming to be black also, often cast down. She had the kind of beauty that Attracta would like one day to possess herself, but knew she would not. Geraldine Carey was like a nun because of the dark clothes she wore, and she had a nun's piety. In the town it was said she couldn't go to Mass often enough. 'Why weren't you a nun, Geraldine?' Attracta asked her once, watching her making bread in her big, cool kitchen. The habit would have suited her, she added, already imagining the housekeeper's face framed by the coif, and the black voluminous skirts. But Geraldine Carey replied that she'd never heard God calling her. 'Only the good are called,' she said.

There'd been a time, faintly remembered Attracta, when her Aunt Emmeline hadn't been well disposed towards Mr. Devereux and Geraldine Carey. There'd been suspicion of some kind, a frowning over the presents he brought, an agitation whenever Attracta was invited to tea. Because of her own excitement over the presents and the invitations Attracta hadn't paid much attention to the nature of her aunt's concern, and looking back on it years later could only speculate. Her Aunt Emmeline was a precise person, a tall woman who had never married, reputed to be delicate. Her house in North Street, very different from Mr. Devereux's, reflected her: it was neat as a new pin, full of light, the windows of its small rooms invariably open at the top to let in fresh air. The fan-light above the hall-door was always gleaming, filling the hall with morning sunlight. Attracta's Aunt Emmeline had a fear of dankness, of damp clothes and wet feet, and rain falling on the head. She worried about lots of things.

Clearly she had worried about Mr. Devereux. There was an occasion when Archdeacon Flower had been specially invited to tea, when Attracta had listened at the sitting-room door because she'd sensed from her aunt's flustered manner that something important was to be discussed. 'Oh, have no worry in that direction at all,' she heard the Archdeacon say. 'Gentle as a lamb that man's become.' Her aunt asked a question Attracta could not hear because of the sound of a tea-cup being replaced on a saucer. 'He's doing the best he can,' the Archdeacon continued, 'according to his lights.' Her aunt mentioned Geraldine Carey, and again the Archdeacon reassured her. 'Bygones are bygones,' he said. 'Isn't it a remarkable thing when a man gets caught in his own snare?' He commented on the quality of her aunt's fruitcake, and then said that everyone should be charitably disposed towards Mr. Devereux and Geraldine Carey. He believed, he said, that that was God's wish.

After that, slowly over the years, Attracta's aunt began to think more highly of Mr. Devereux, until in the end there was no one in the entire town, with the possible exception of Archdeacon Flower, whom she held in greater esteem. Once when Phelan the coal merchant insisted that she hadn't paid for half a ton of coal and she recollected perfectly giving the money to the man who'd delivered it, Mr. Devereux had come to her aid. 'A right old devil, Phelan is,' Attracta heard him saying in the hall, and that was the end her aunt had ever heard of the matter. On Saturday evenings, having kept Attracta company on her walk home, Mr. Devereux might remain for a little while in the house in North Street. He sometimes brought lettuces or cuttings with him, or tomatoes or strawberries. He would take a glass of sherry in the trim little sitting-room with its delicate inlaid chairs that matched the delicacy of Attracta's aunt. Often he'd still be there, taking a second glass, when Attracta came down to say goodnight. Her aunt's cat Diggory liked to climb up on to his knees, and as if in respect of some kind Mr. Devereux never lit his pipe. He and her aunt would converse in low voices and generally they'd cease when Attracta entered the room. She would kiss him goodnight after she'd kissed her aunt. She imagined it was what having a father was like.

*

At the town's approximate centre there stood a grey woman, on a pedestal, a statute of the Maid of Erin. It was here, only yards from this monument, that Mr. Purce told Attracta the truth about her parents' death, when she was eleven. She'd always had the feeling that Mr. Purce wanted to speak to her, even that he was waiting until she could understand what it was he had to say. He was a man people didn't much like; he'd settled in the town, having come there from somewhere else. He was a clerk in the court-house.

'There's a place I know where there's greenfinches,' he said, as if introducing himself. 'Ten nests of them, maybe twelve, maybe more. D'you understand me, Attracta? Would you like me to show you?'

She was on her way home from school. She had to get back to do her homework, she said to Mr. Purce. She didn't want to go looking for greenfinches with him.

'Did Devereux tell you not to talk to Mr. Purce?' he said, and she shook her head. As far as she could remember, Mr. Devereux had never mentioned Mr. Purce. 'I see you in church,' Mr. Purce said.

She had seen him too, sitting in the front, over on the left-hand side. Her aunt had often remarked that the day Mr. Purce didn't go to church it would be a miracle. It was like Geraldine Carey going to Mass.

'I'll walk out with you,' he said. 'I have a half-day today for myself.'

They walked together, to her embarrassment. She glanced at shop-windows to catch a glimpse of their reflec-

111

tion, to see if they looked as awkward as she felt. He was
only a head taller than she and part of that was made up by
his hard black hat. His clerk's suit was double-breasted,
navy-blue with a pale stripe in it, shiny here and there, in
need of a good ironing. He wore black leather gloves and
carried a walking-stick. He always had the gloves and the
walking-stick in church, but his Sunday suit was superior
to the one he wore now. Her own fair hair, pinned up under her green-brimmed hat, was what stood out between
the two of them. The colour of good corn, Mr. Devereux
used to say, and she always considered that a compliment,
coming from a grain merchant. Her face was thin and her
eyes blue, but reflected in the shop windows there was
now only a blur of flesh, a thin shaft between her hat and
the green coat that matched it.

'You've had misfortune, Attracta.' Solemnly he nodded,
repeating the motion of his head until she wished he'd
stop. 'It was a terrible thing to be killed by mistake.'

Attracta didn't know what he was talking about. They
passed by the last of the shops in North Street, Shannon's
grocery and bar, O'Brien's bakery, the hardware that
years ago had run out of stock. The narrow street widened
a bit. Mr. Purce said:

'Has she made a Catholic girl out of you, Attracta?'

'Who, Mr. Purce?'

'Devereux's woman. Has she tried anything on? Has she
shown you rosary beads?'

She shook her head.

'Don't ever look at them if she does. Look away immediately if she gets them out of her apron or anything
like that. Will you promise me that, girl?'

'I don't think she would. I don't think, Mr. Devereux
—'

'You can never tell with that crowd. There isn't a trick
in the book they won't hop on to. Will you promise me
now? Have nothing to do with carry-on like that.'

'Yes, Mr. Purce.'

As they walked he prodded at the litter on the pavement

112

with his walking-stick. Cigarette packets and squashed match-boxes flew into the gutter, bits of the *Cork Examiner*, sodden paper-bags. He was known for this activity in the town and even when he was on his own his voice was often heard protesting at the untidiness.

'I'm surprised they never told you, Attracta,' he said. 'What are you now, girl?'

'I'm eleven.'

'A big girl should know things like that.'

'What things, Mr. Purce?'

He nodded in his repetitious manner, and then he explained himself. The tragedy had occurred in darkness, at night: her parents had accidentally become involved with an ambush meant for the Black and Tan soldiers who were in force in the area at the time. She herself had long since been asleep at home, and as he spoke she remembered waking up to find herself in a bed in her aunt's house, without knowing how she got there. 'That's how they got killed, Attracta,' Mr. Purce said, and then he said an extraordinary thing. 'You've got Devereux and his woman to thank for it.'

She knew that the Black and Tan soldiers had been camped near the town; she knew there'd been fighting. She realised that the truth about the death had been counted too terrible for a child to bear. But that her parents should have been shot, and shot in error, that the whole thing had somehow been the responsibility of Mr. Devereux and Geraldine Carey, seemed inconceivable to Attracta.

'They destroyed a decent Protestant pair,' Mr. Purce continued, still flicking litter from the pavement. 'Half-ten at night on a public road, destroyed like pests.'

The sun, obscured by clouds while Attracta and Mr. Purce had made the journey from the centre of the town, was suddenly warm on Attracta's face. A woman in a horse and cart, attired in the black hooded cloak of the locality, passed slowly by. There were sacks of meal in the cart which had probably come from Mr. Devereux's mill.

'Do you understand what I'm saying to you, Attracta? Devereux was organising resistance up in the hills. He had explosives and booby traps, he was drilling men to go and kill people. Did nobody tell you about himself and Geraldine Carey?'

She shook her head. He nodded again, as if to indicate that little better could be expected.

'Listen to me, Attracta. Geraldine Carey was brought into this town by the man she got married to, who used to work at Devereux's mill. Six months later she'd joined up with Devereux in the type of dirty behaviour I wouldn't soil myself telling you about. Not only that, Attracta, she was gun-running with him. She was fixing explosives like a man would, dressed up like a man in uniform. Devereux was as wild as a savage. There was nothing Devereux wouldn't do, there was nothing the woman wouldn't do either. They'd put booby traps down and it didn't matter who got killed. They'd ambush the British soldiers when the soldiers didn't have a chance.'

It was impossible to believe him. It was impossible to visualise the housekeeper and Mr. Devereux in the role he'd given them. No one with any sense could believe that Geraldine Carey would kill people. Was everything Mr. Purce said a lie? He was a peculiar man: had he some reason for stating her mother and her father had met their deaths in this way?

'Your father was a decent man, Attracta. He was never drunk in his life. There was prayers for him in the chapel, but that was only a hypocrisy of the priests. Wouldn't the priest Quinn like to see every Protestant in this town dead and buried? Wouldn't he like to see you and me six feet down with clay in our eye-sockets?'

Attracta didn't believe that, and more certainly now it seemed to her that everything Mr. Purce said was untrue. Catholics were different; they crossed themselves when they passed their chapel; they went in for crosses and con- fession; they had Masses and candles. But it was hard to ac- cept that Father Quinn, a jovial red-faced man, would prefer it if she were dead. She'd heard her aunt's maid Philomena saying that Father Doran was cantankerous and that Father Martin wasn't worth his salt, but neither of them seemed to Attracta to be the kind of man who'd wish people dead. 'Proddy-woddy green-guts,' Catholic children would shout out sometimes. 'Catty Catty going to Mass,' the Protestants would reply, 'riding on the Devil's ass.' But there was never much vindictiveness about any of it. The sides were unevenly matched: there were too few Protestants in the town to make a proper opposition; trouble was avoided.

'He was a traitor to his religion, Attracta. And I'll promise you this: if I was to tell you about that woman of his you wouldn't enter the house they have.' Abruptly he turned and walked away, back into the town, his walking-stick still frantically working, poking at any litter it could find.

The sun was hot now. Attracta felt sticky within her several layers of clothes. She had a chapter of her history book to read, about the Saxons coming to England. She had four long-division sums to do, and seven lines of poetry to learn. *What potions have I drunk of Syren tears*, the first one stated, a statement Attracta could make neither head nor tail of.

She didn't go straight home. Instead she turned off to the left and walked through a back street, out into the country. She passed fields of mangels and turnips, again trying to imagine the scenes Mr. Purce had sketched for her, the ambush of men waiting for the soldiers, the firing of shots. It occurred to her that she had never asked anyone if her parents were buried in the Church of Ireland graveyard.

She passed by tinkers encamped on the verge of the road. A woman ran after her and asked for money, saying her husband had just died. She swore when Attracta said she hadn't any, and then her manner changed again. She developed a whine in her voice, she said she'd pray for Attracta if she'd bring her money, tomorrow or the next day.

Had Mr. Purce only wished to turn her against Mr.

Devereux because Mr. Devereux did not go to church? Was there no more to it than that? Did Mr. Purce say the first thing that came into his head? As Attracta walked, the words of Archdeacon Flower came back to her: in stating that Mr. Devereux was now as gentle as a lamb, was there the implication that once he hadn't been? And had her aunt, worried about Geraldine Carey, been reassured on that score also?

'It's all over now, dear,' her aunt said. She looked closely at Attracta and then put her arms round her, as if expecting tears. But tears didn't come, for Attracta was only amazed.

*

Fifty years later, walking through the heather by the sea, Attracta remembered vividly that moment of her childhood. She couldn't understand how Mr. Devereux and Geraldine Carey had changed so. 'Maybe they bear the burden of guilt,' Archdeacon Flower had explained, summoned to the house the following day by her aunt. 'Maybe they look at you and feel responsible. It was an accident, but people can feel responsible for an accident.' What had happened was in the past, he reminded her, as her aunt had. She understood what they were implying, that it must all be forgotten, yet she couldn't help imagining Mr. Devereux and his housekeeper laying booby traps on roads and drilling men in the hills. Geraldine Carey's husband had left the town, Mr. Purce told her on a later occasion: he'd gone to Co. Louth and handn't been heard of since. 'Whore,' Mr. Purce said. 'No better than a whore she is.' Attracta, looking the word up in a dictionary, was astonished.

Having started, Mr. Purce went on and on. Mr. Devereux's house wasn't suitable for an eleven-year-old girl to visit, since it was the house of a murderer. Wasn't it a disgrace that a Protestant girl should set foot in a house where the deaths of British soldiers and the Protestant Irish had been planned? One Saturday afternoon, unable to restrain himself, he arrived at the house himself. He shouted at Mr. Devereux from the open hall-door. 'Isn't it enough to have destroyed her father and mother without letting that woman steal her for the Pope?' His grey face was suffused with pink beneath his hard hat, his walking-stick thrashed the air. Mr. Devereux called him an Orange mason. 'I hate the bloody sight of you,' Mr. Purce said in a quieter voice, and then in his abrupt way he walked off.

That, too, Attracta remembered as she continued her walk around the headland. Mr. Devereux afterwards never referred to it, and Mr. Purce never spoke to her again, as if deciding that there was nothing left to say. In the town as she grew up people would reluctantly answer her when she questioned them about her parents' tragedy in an effort to discover more than her aunt or Archdeacon Flower had revealed. But nothing new emerged, the people she asked only agreeing that Mr. Devereux in those days had been as wild as Mr. Purce suggested. He'd drilled the local men, he'd been assisted in every way by Geraldine Carey, whose husband had gone away to Co. Louth. But everything had been different since the night of the tragedy.

Her aunt tried to explain to her the nature of Mr. Purce's hatred of Mr. Devereux. Mr. Purce saw things in a certain light, she said, he could not help himself. He couldn't help believing that Father Quinn would prefer the town's Protestants to be dead and buried. He couldn't help believing that immorality continued in the relationship between Mr. Devereux and his housekeeper when clearly it did not. He found a spark and made a fire of it, he was a bigot and was unable to do anything about it. The Protestants of the town felt ashamed of him.

Mr. Purce died, and was said to have continued in his hatred with his last remaining breaths. He mentioned the Protestant girl, his bleak, harsh voice weakening. She had been contaminated and infected, she was herself no better than the people who used her for their evil purposes. She was not fit to teach the Protestant children of the town, as

117

she was now commencing to do. 'As I lie dying,' Mr. Purce said to the clergyman who had succeeded Archdeacon Flower, 'I am telling you that, sir.' But afterwards, when the story of Mr. Purce's death went round, the people of the town looked at Attracta with a certain admiration, seeming to suggest that for her the twisting of events had not been easy, neither the death of her parents nor the forgiveness asked of her by Mr. Devereux, nor the bigotry of Mr. Purce. She'd been caught in the middle of things, they seemed to suggest, and had survived unharmed.

Surviving, she was happy in the town. Too happy to marry the exchange clerk from the Provincial Bank or the young man who came on a holiday to Cedarstrand with his parents. *Pride goeth before destruction*, her pupils' headlines stated, and *Look before you leap*. Their fingers pressed hard on inky pens, knuckles jutting beneath the strain, tongue-tips aiding concentration. Ariadne, Finn Mac Cool, King Arthur's sword, Cathleen ni Houlihan: legends filled the schoolroom, with facts about the Romans and the Normans, square roots and the Gulf Stream. Children grew up and went away, returning sometimes to visit Attracta in her house in North Street. Others remained and in the town she watched them changing, grey coming into their hair, no longer moving as lithely as they had. She developed an affection for the town without knowing why, beyond the fact that it was part of her.

'Yet in all a lifetime I learn nothing,' she said aloud to herself on the headland. 'And I taught nothing either.' She gazed out at the smooth blue Atlantic but did not see it clearly. She saw instead the brown-paper parcel that contained the biscuit-box she had read about, and the fingers of Penelope Vade undoing the string and the brown paper. She saw her lifting off the lid. She saw her frowning for a moment, before the eyes of the man she loved stared deadly into hers. Months later, all courage spent, defeated in her gesture, the body of Penelope Vade dragged itself across the floors of two different rooms. There was the

118

bottle full of aspirins in a cupboard, and water drunk from a Wedgewood-patterned cup, like the cups Attracta drank from every day.

*

In her schoolroom, with its maps and printed pictures, the sixteen faces stared at her, the older children at the back. She repeated her question.

'Now, what does anyone think of that?'

Again she read them the news item, reading it slowly because she wanted it to become as rooted in their minds as it was in hers. She lingered over the number of bullets that had been fired into the body of Penelope Vade's husband, and over the removal of his head.

'Can you see that girl? Can you imagine men putting a human head in a tin box and sending it through the post? Can you imagine her receiving it? The severed head of the man she loved?'

'Sure, isn't there stuff like that in the papers the whole time?' one of the children suggested.

She agreed that that was so. 'I've had a good life in this town,' she added, and the children looked at her as if she'd suddenly turned mad.

'I'm getting out of it,' one of them said after a pause. 'Back of beyond, miss.'

She began at the beginning. She tried to get into the children's minds an image of a baby sleeping while violence and death took place on the Cork road. She described her Aunt Emmeline's house in North Street, the neat feminine house it had been, her aunt's cat Diggory, the small sittingroom, her aunt's maid Philomena. She spoke of her own very fair hair and her thin face, and the heavy old-fashioned clothes she'd worn in those days. She spoke of the piety of Geraldine Carey, and the grain merchant's tired face. The friendship they offered her was like Penelope Vade proclaiming peace in the city where her husband had been killed; it was a gesture, too.

'His house would smell of roses on a summer's day. She'd carry his meals to him, coming out of the shadows of her kitchen. As if in mourning, the blue blinds darkened the drawing-room. It was they who bore the tragedy, not I.'

She described Mr. Purce's face and his grating voice. She tried to make of him a figure they could see among the houses and shops that were familiar to them: the hard black hat, the walking-stick poking away litter. He had done his best to rescue her, acting according to his beliefs. He wanted her not to forget, not realising that there was nothing for her to remember.

'But I tried to imagine,' she said, 'as I am asking you to imagine now: my mother and father shot dead on the Cork road, and Mr. Devereux and Geraldine Carey as two monstrous people, and arms being blown off soldiers, and vengeance breeding vengeance.'

A child raised a hand and asked to leave the room. Attracta gave permission and awaited the child's return before proceeding. She filled the time in by describing things that had changed in the town, the falling to pieces of O'Mara's Picture House, the closing of the tannery in 1938. When the child came back she told of Mr. Purce's death, how he'd said she was not fit to teach Protestant children.

'I tried to imagine a night I'd heard about,' she said, 'when Mr. Devereux's men found a man in Madden's public house whom they said had betrayed them, and how they took him out to Cedarstrand and hanged him in a barn. Were they pleased after they'd done that? Did they light cigarettes, saying the man was better dead? One of those other men must have gone to a post office with the wrapped biscuit-box. He must have watched it being weighed and paid the postage. Did he say to himself he was exceptional to have hoodwinked a post-office clerk?'

Obediently listening in their rows of worn desks, the children wondered what on earth all this was about. No geography or history lesson had ever been so bewildering;

those who found arithmetic difficult would have settled for attempting to understand it now. They watched the lined face of their teacher, still thin as she'd said it had been in childhood, the fair hair grey now. The mouth twitched and rapidly moved, seeming sometimes to quiver as if it struggled against tears. What on earth had this person called Penelope Vade to do with anything?

'She died believing that hell had come already. She'd lost all faith in human life, and who can blame her? She might have stayed in Haslemere, like anyone else would have. Was she right to go to the city where her husband had been murdered, to show its other victims that her spirit had not been wholly crushed?'

No one answered, and Attracta was aware of the children's startled gaze. But the startled gaze was a natural reaction. She said to herself that it didn't matter.

'My story is one with hers,' she said. 'Horror stories, with different endings only. I think of her now and I can see quite clearly the flat she lived in in Belfast. I can see the details, correctly or not I've no idea. Wallpaper with a pattern of brownish purple flowers on it, gaunt furniture casting shadows, a tea-caddy on the hired television set. I drag my body across the floors of two rooms, over a carpet that smells of dust and cigarette ash, over rugs and cool linoleum. I reach up in the kitchen, a hand on the edge of the sink: one by one I eat the aspirins until the bottle's empty.'

There was a silence. Feet were shuffled in the schoolroom. No one spoke.

'If only she had known,' Attracta said, 'that there was still a faith she might have had, that God does not forever withhold His mercy. Will those same men who exacted that vengeance on her one day keep bees and budgerigars? Will they serve in shops, and be kind to the blind and the deaf? Will they garden in the evenings and be good fathers? It is not impossible. Oh, can't you see,' she cried, 'what happened in this town? Here, at the back of beyond. Can't you appreciate it? And can't you see her lying there, mice nibbling her dried blood?'

The children still were quiet, their faces still not registering the comment she wished to make. It was because she'd been clumsy, she thought. All she'd meant to tell them was never to despair. All she had meant to do was to prepare them for a future that looked grim. She had been happy, she said again. The conversation of Mr. Purce had been full of the truth but it hadn't made sense because the years had turned the truth around.

To the children she appeared to be talking now to herself. She was old, a few of them said to themselves; that was it. She didn't appear to understand that almost every day there was the kind of vengeance she spoke of reported on the television. Bloodshed was wholesale, girls were tarred and left for dead, children no older than they were armed with guns.

'I only hope,' they heard her saying, 'she knows that strangers mourn her.'

Another silence lingered awkwardly and then she nodded at a particular child and the child rose and rang a hand-bell. The children filed away, well-mannered and docile as she had taught them to be. She watched them in the playground, standing in twos and threes, talking about her. It had meant nothing when she'd said that people change. The gleam of hope she'd offered had been too slight to be of use, irrelevant in the horror they took for granted, as part of life. Yet she could not help still believing that it mattered when monsters did not remain monsters for ever. It wasn't much to put against the last bleak moments of Penelope Vade, but it was something for all that. She wished she could have made her point.

Twenty minutes later, when the children returned to the schoolroom, her voice no longer quivered, nor did it seem to struggle against tears. The older children learnt about agriculture in Sweden, the younger ones about the Pyrenees, the youngest that Munster had six counties. The day came to an end at three o'clock and when all the children had gone Attracta locked the schoolroom and walked to the house she had inherited in North Street.

A week later Archdeacon Flower's successor came to see her, his visit interrupting further violence on the television news. He beat about the bush while he nibbled biscuits and drank cups of tea by the fire; then he suggested that perhaps she should consider retiring one of these days. She was over sixty, he pointed out with his clerical laugh, and she replied that Mr. Ayrie had gone on until seventy. Sixty, the clergyman repeated with another laugh, was the post's retirement age. Children were a handful nowadays.

She smiled, thinking of her sixteen docile charges. They had chattered to their parents, and the parents had been shocked to hear that they'd been told of a man decapitated and a girl raped seven times. School was not for that, they had angrily protested to the clergyman, and he had had no option but to agree. At the end of the summer term there'd be a presentation of Waterford glass.

'Every day in my schoolroom I should have honoured the small, remarkable thing that happened in this town. It matters that she died in despair, with no faith left in human life.'

He was brisk. For as long as most people could remember she had been a remarkable teacher; in no way had she failed. He turned the conversation to more cheerful topics, he ate more biscuits and a slice of cake. He laughed and even made a joke. He retailed a little harmless gossip.

Eventually she stood up. She walked with her visitor to the hall, shook hands with him and saw him out. In the sitting-room she piled the tea things on to a tray and placed it on a table by the door. She turned the television on again but when the screen lit up she didn't notice it. The face of Penelope Vade came into her mind, the smile a little crooked, the freckled cheeks.

The Death of Peggy Morrissey

Like all children, I led a double life. There was the
ordinariness of dressing in the morning, putting on shoes
and combing hair, stirring a spoon through porridge I
didn't want, and going at ten-to-nine to the nuns' elementary school. And there was a world in which only the
events I wished for happened, where boredom was not
permitted and of which I was both God and King.

In my ordinary life I was the only child of parents who
years before my birth had given up hope of ever having
me. I remember them best as being different from other
parents: they were elderly, it seemed to me, two greyly
fussing people with grey hair and faces, in grey clothes,
with spectacles. 'Oh, no, no,' they murmured regularly,
rejecting on my behalf an invitation to tea or to play with
some other child. They feared on my behalf the rain and
the sea, and walls that might be walked along, and grass
because grass was always damp. They rarely missed a service at the Church of the Holy Assumption.

In the town where we lived, a seaside town thirty miles
from Cork, my father was employed as a senior clerk in
the offices of Devereux and O'Brien, Solicitors and Com-
missioners for Oaths. With him on one side of me and my
mother on the other, we walked up and down the brief
promenade in winter, while the seagulls shrieked and my
father worried in case it was going to rain. We never went
for walks through fields or through the heathery
wastelands that sloped gently upwards behind the town, or
by the river where people said Sir Walter Raleigh had
fished. In summer, when the visitors from Cork came, my

mother didn't like to let me near the sands because the sands, she said, were full of fleas. In summer we didn't walk on the promenade but out along the main Cork road instead, past a house that appeared to me to move. It disappeared for several minutes as we approached it, a trick of nature, I afterwards discovered, caused by the undulations of the landscape. Every July, for a fortnight, we went to stay in Montenotte, high up above Cork City, in a boarding-house run by my mother's sister, my Aunt Isabella. She, too, had a grey look about her and was religious.

It was here, in my Aunt Isabella's Montenotte boarding-house, that this story begins: in the summer of 1936, when I was seven. It was a much larger house than the one we lived in ourselves, which was small and narrow and in a terrace. My Aunt Isabella's was rather grand in its way, a dark place with little unexpected half-landings, and badly lit corridors. It smelt of floor polish and of mustiness that I have since associated with the religious life, a smell of old cassocks. Everywhere there were statues of the Virgin, and votive lights and black-framed pictures of the Holy Child. The residents were all priests, old and middle-aged and young, eleven of them usually, which was all the house would hold. A few were always away on their holidays when we stayed there in the summer.

In the summer of 1936 we left our own house in the usual way, my father fastening all the windows and the front and back doors and then examining the house from the outside to make sure he'd done the fastening and the locking properly. We walked to the railway station, each of us carrying something, my mother a brown cardboard suitcase and my father a larger one of the same kind. I carried the sandwiches we were to have on the train, and a flask of carefully made tea and three apples, all packed into a sixpenny fish basket.

In the house in Montenotte my Aunt Isabella told us that Canon Maguire and Father Quinn were on holiday, one in Tralee, the other in Galway. She led us to their rooms,

Canon Maguire's for my father and Father Quinn's for my mother and myself. The familiar trestle-bed was erected at the foot of the bed in my mother's room. During the course of the year a curate called Father Ryan had repaired it, my aunt said, after it had been used by Canon Maguire's brother from America, who'd proved too much for the canvas.

'Ah, aren't you looking well, Mr. Mahon!' the red-faced and jolly Father Smith said to my father in the dining-room that evening. 'And isn't our friend here getting big for himself?' He laughed loudly, gripping a portion of the back of my neck between a finger and a thumb. Did I know my catechism? he asked me. Was I being good with the nuns in the elementary school? 'Are you in health yourself, Mrs. Mahon?' he inquired of my mother.

My mother said she was, and the red-faced priest went to join the other priests at the main dining-table. He left behind him a smell that was different from the smell of the house, and I noticed that he had difficulty in pulling the chair out from the table when he was about to sit down. He had to be assisted in this by a new young curate, a Father Parsloe. Father Smith had been drinking stout again, I said to myself.

Sometimes in my aunt's house there was nothing to do except to watch and to listen. Father Smith used to drink too much stout; Father Maginnis, who was so thin you could hardly bear to look at him and whose flesh was the colour of whitewash, was not long for this world; Father Riordon would be a bishop if only he could have tidied himself up a bit; Canon Maguire had once refused to baptise a child; young Father Ryan was going places. For hours on end my Aunt Isabella would murmur to my parents about the priests, telling about the fate of one who had left the boarding-house during the year or supplying background information about a new one. My parents, so faultlessly regular in their church attendance and interested in all religious matters, were naturally pleased to listen. God and the organisation of His Church were far more important than my father's duties in Devereux and O'Brien, or my mother's housework, or my own desire to go walking through heathery wastelands that sloped gently upwards behind our town. God and the priests in my Aunt Isabella's house, and the nuns of the convent elementary school and the priests of the Church of the Holy Assumption, were at the centre of everything. 'Maybe it'll appeal to our friend.' Father Smith had once said in the dining-room, and I knew that he meant that maybe one day I might be attracted towards the priesthood. My parents had not said anything in reply, but as we ate our tea of sausages and potato-cakes I could feel them thinking that nothing would please them better.

Every year when we stayed with my aunt there was an afternoon when I was left in charge of whichever priests happened to be in, while my parents and my aunt made the journey across the city to visit my father's brother, who was a priest himself. There was some difficulty about bringing me: I had apparently gone to my uncle's house as a baby, when my presence had upset him. Years later I overheard my mother whispering to Father Riordon about this, suggesting – or so it seemed – that my father had once been intent on the priestly life but had at the last moment withdrawn. That he should afterwards have fathered a child was apparently an offence to his brother's feeling of propriety. I had the impression that my uncle was a severe man, who looked severely on my father and my mother and my Aunt Isabella on these visits, and was respected by them for being as he was. All three came back subdued, and that night my mother always prayed for much longer by the side of her bed.

'Father Parsloe's going to take you for a walk,' my Aunt Isabella said on the morning of the 1936 visit. 'He wants to get to know you.'

You walked all the way down from Montenotte, past the docks, over the river and into the city. The first few times it could have been interesting, but after that it was worse than walking on the concrete promenade at home.

I'd have far preferred to have played by myself in my aunt's overgrown back garden, pretending to be grown up, talking to myself in a secret way, having wicked thoughts. At home and in my aunt's garden I became a man my father had read about in a newspaper and whom, he'd said, we must all pray for, a thief who broke the windows of jewellers' shops and lifted out watches and rings. I became Father Smith, drinking too much stout and missing the steps of the stairs. I became Father Maginnis and would lie on the weeds at the bottom of the garden or under a table, confessing to gruesome crimes at the moment of death. In my mind I mocked the holiness of my parents and imitated their voices; I mocked the holiness of my Aunt Isabella; I talked back to my parents in a way I never would. I laughed and said disgraceful things about God and the religious life. Blasphemy was exciting.

'Are you ready so?' Father Parsloe said when my aunt had left for the visit to my uncle. 'Will we take a bus?'

'A bus?'

'Down to the town.'

I'd never in my life done that before. The buses were for going longer distances in. It seemed extraordinary not to walk, the whole point of a walk was to walk.

'I have't any money for the bus.' I said, and Father Parsloe laughed. On the upper deck he lit a cigarette. He was a slight young man, by far the youngest of the priests in my aunt's house, with reddish hair and a face that seemed to be on a slant. 'Will we have tea in Thompson's?' he said. 'Would that be a good thing to do?'

We had tea in Thompson's café, with buns and cakes and huge meringues such as I'd never tasted before. Father Parsloe smoked fourteen cigarettes and drank all the tea himself. I had three bottles of fizzy orangeade. 'Will we go to the pictures?' Father Parsloe said when he'd paid the bill at the cash desk. 'Will we chance the Pavilion?'

I had never, of course, been to the pictures before. My mother said that Horgan's Picture-House, which was the only one in our town, was full of fleas.

'One and a half,' Father Parsloe said at the cash desk in the Pavilion and we were led away into the darkness. THE END it announced on the screen, and when I saw it I thought we were too late. 'Ah, aren't we in lovely time?' Father Parsloe said.

I didn't understand the film. It was about grown-ups kissing one another, and about an earthquake, and then a motor-car accident in which a woman who'd been kissed a lot was killed. The man who'd kissed her was married to another woman, and when the film ended he was sitting in a room with his wife, looking at her. She kept saying it was all right.

'God, wasn't that great?' Father Parsloe said as we stood in the lavatory of the Pavilion, the kind of lavatory where you stand up, like I'd never been in before. 'Wasn't it a good story?'

All the way back to Montenotte I kept remembering it. I kept seeing the face of the woman who'd been killed, and all the bodies lying on the streets after the earthquake, and the man at the end, sitting in a room with his wife. The swaying of the bus made me feel queasy because of the meringues and the orangeade, but I didn't care.

'Did you enjoy the afternoon?' Father Parsloe asked, and I told him I'd never enjoyed anything better. I asked him if the pictures were always as good. He assured me they were.

My parents, however, didn't seem pleased. My father got hold of a *Cork Examiner* and looked up the film that was on at the Pavilion and reported that it wasn't suitable for a child. My mother gave me a bath and examined my clothes for fleas. When Father Parsloe winked at me in the dining-room my parents pretended not to notice him.

That night my mother prayed for her extra long period, after the visit to my uncle. I lay in the dimly lit room, aware that she was kneeling there, but thinking of the film and the way the people had kissed, not like my parents had ever kissed. At the convent elementary school there were girls in the higher classes who were pretty, far prettier than my mother. There was one called Claire, with fair hair and a softly freckled face, and another called Peggy Morrissey, who was younger and black-haired. I had picked them out because they had spoken to me, asking my name; I thought them very nice.

I opened my eyes and saw that my mother was rising from her knees. She stood for a moment at the edge of her bed, not smiling, her lips still moving, continuing her prayer. Then she got into bed and put out the light.

I listened to her breathing and heard it become the breathing which people have when they're asleep, but I couldn't sleep myself. I lay there, still remembering the film and remembering being in Thompson's and seeing Father Parsloe lighting one cigarette after another. For some reason, I began to imagine that I was in Thompson's with Father Parsloe and the two girls from the convent, and that we all went off to the Pavilion together, swinging along the street. 'Ah, isn't this the life for us?' Father Parsloe said as he led us into the darkness, and I told the girls I'd been to the Pavilion before and they said they never had.

I heard eleven o'clock chiming from a nearby church. I heard a stumbling on the stairs and then the laughter of Father Smith, and Father Riordon telling him to be quiet. I heard twelve chiming and half-past twelve, and a quarter-to-one, and one.

After that I didn't want to sleep. I was standing in a classroom of the convent and Claire was smiling at me. It was nice being with her. I felt warm all over, and happy.

And then I was walking on the sands with Peggy Morrissey. We ran, playing a game she'd made up, and then we walked again. She asked if I'd like to go on a picnic with her, next week perhaps.

I didn't know what to do. I wanted one of the girls to be my friend. I wanted to love one of them, like the people had loved in the film. I wanted to kiss one and be with one, just the two of us. In the darkness of the bedroom they both seemed close and real, closer than my mother, even

130

though I could hear my mother breathing. 'Come on,' Peggy Morrissey whispered, and then Claire whispered also, saying we'd always be best friends, saying we might run away. It was all wrong that there were two of them, yet both vividly remained. 'Tuesday,' Peggy Morrissey said. 'We'll have the picnic on Tuesday.'

Her father drove us in his car, away from the town. out beyond the heathery wastelands, towards a hillside that was even nicer. But a door of the car, the back door against which Peggy Morrissey was leaning, suddenly gave way. On the dust of the road she was as dead as the woman in the film.

'Poor Peggy,' Claire said at some later time, even though she hadn't known Peggy Morrissey very well. 'Poor little Peggy.' And then she smiled and took my hand and we walked together through the heathery wastelands, in love with one another.

A few days later we left my Aunt Isabella's house in Montenotte and returned on the train to our seaside town. And a week after that a new term began at the convent elementary school. Peggy Morrissey was dead, the Reverend Mother told us, all of us assembled together. She added that there was diphtheria in the town.

I didn't think about it at first; and I didn't connect the reality of the death with a fantasy that had been caused by my first visit to a cinema. Some part of my mind may passingly have paused over the coincidence, but that was all. There was the visit to the Pavilion itself to talk about in the convent, and the description of the film, and Father Parsloe's conversation and the way he'd smoked fourteen cigarettes in Thompson's. Diphtheria was a terrible disease, my mother said when I told her, and naturally we must all pray for the soul of poor Peggy Morrissey.

But as weeks and months went by, I found myself increasingly remembering the story I had told myself on the night of the film, and remembering particularly how Peggy Morrissey had fallen from the car, and how she'd looked when she was dead. I said to myself that that had been my wickedest thought, worse than my blasphemies and yet somehow part of them. At night I lay in bed, unable to sleep, trying hopelessly to pray for forgiveness. But no forgiveness came, for there was no respite to the images that recurred, her face in life and then in death, like the face of the woman in the film.

A year later, while lying awake in the same room in my aunt's boarding-house, I saw her. In the darkness there was a sudden patch of light and in the centre of it she was wearing a sailor-suit that I remembered. Her black plaits hung down her back. She smiled at me and went away. I knew instinctively then, as I watched her and after she'd gone, that the fantasy and the reality were part and parcel: I had caused this death to occur.

Looking back on it now, I can see, of course, that that feeling was a childish one. It was a childish fear, a superstition that occurring to an adult would cause only a shiver of horror. But, as a child, with no one to consult about the matter, I lived with the thought that my will was more potent than I knew. In stories I had learnt of witches and spells and evil spirits, and power locked up in people. In my games I had wickedly denied the religious life, and goodness, and holiness. In my games I had mocked Father Smith; I had pretended that the dying Father Maginnis was a criminal. I had pretended to be a criminal myself, a man who broke jewellers' windows. I had imitated my parents when it said you should honour your father and your mother. I had mocked the holiness of my Aunt Isabella. I had murdered Peggy Morrissey because there wasn't room for her in the story I was telling myself. I was possessed and evil; the nuns had told us about people being like that.

I thought at first I might seek advice from Father Parsloe. I thought of asking him if he remembered the day we'd gone on our outing, and then telling him how, in a story I was telling myself, I'd caused Peggy Morrissey to be killed in a car accident like the woman in the film, and how she'd died in reality, of diphtheria. But Father Parsloe had an impatient kind of look about him this year, as if he had worries of his own. So I didn't tell him and I didn't tell anyone. I hoped that when we returned to our own house at the end of the stay in Montenotte I wouldn't see her again, but the very first day we were back I saw her at four o'clock in the afternoon, in the kitchen.

After that she came irregularly, sometimes not for a month and once not for a year. She continued to appear in the same sudden way but in different clothes, and growing up as I was growing up. Once, after I'd left the convent and gone on to the Christian Brothers, she appeared in the classroom, smiling near the blackboard.

She never spoke. Whether she appeared on the promenade or at school or in my aunt's house or our house, close to me or at a distance, she communicated only with her smile and with her eyes: I was possessed of the Devil, she came herself from God. In her eyes and her smile there was that simple message, a message which said also that my thoughts were always wicked, that I had never believed properly in God or the Virgin or Jesus who died for us.

I tried to pray. Like my mother, kneeling beside my bed. Like my aunt and her houseful of priests. Like the nuns and Christian Brothers, and other boys and girls of the town. But prayer would not come to me, and I realised that it never had. I had always pretended, going down on my knees at Mass, laughing and blaspheming in my mind. I hated the very thought of prayer. I hated my parents in an unnatural manner, and my Aunt Isabella and the priests in her house. But the dead Peggy Morrissey, fresh from God's heaven, was all forgiveness in her patch of light, smiling to rid me of my evil spirit.

She was there at my mother's funeral, and later at my father's. Claire, whom I had destroyed her for, married a man employed in the courthouse and became a Mrs. Madden, prematurely fat. I naturally didn't marry anyone

133

myself.

I am forty-six years old now and I live alone in the same seaside town. No one in the town knows why I am solitary. No one could guess that I have lived with a child's obsession for half a lifetime. Being no longer a child, I naturally no longer believe that I was responsible for the death. In my passing, careless fantasy I wished for it and she, already dead, picked up my living thoughts. I should not have wished for it because in middle age she is a beautiful creature now, more beautiful by far than fat Mrs. Madden.

And that is all there is. At forty-six I walk alone on the brief promenade, or by the edge of the sea or on the road to Cork, where the moving house is. I work, as my father worked, in the offices of Devereux and O'Brien. I cook my own food. I sleep alone in a bed that has an iron bedstead. On Sundays I go hypocritically to Mass in the Church of the Holy Assumption; I go to Confession and do not properly confess; I go to Men's Confraternity, and to Communion. And all the time she is there, appearing in her patch of light to remind me that she never leaves me. And all the time, on my knees at Mass, or receiving the Body and the Blood, or in my iron bed, I desire her. In the offices of Devereux and O'Brien I dream of her nakedness. When we are old I shall desire her, too, with my shrunken, evil body.

In the town I am a solitary, peculiar man. I have been rendered so, people probably say, by my cloistered upbringing, and probably add that such an upbringing would naturally cultivate a morbid imagination. That may be so, and it doesn't really matter how things have come about. All I know is that she is more real for me than anything else is in this seaside town or beyond it. I live for her, living hopelessly, for I know I can never possesses her as I wish to. I have a carnal desire for a shadow, which in turn is His mockery of me: His fitting punishment for my wickedest thought of all.

Miss Smith

One day Miss Smith asked James what a baby horse was called and James couldn't remember. He blinked and shook his head. He knew, he explained, but he just couldn't remember. Miss Smith said:

'Well, well, James Machen doesn't know what a baby horse is called.'

She said it loudly so that everyone in the class-room heard. James became very confused. He blinked and said:

'Pony, Miss Smith?'

'Pony! James Machen says a baby horse is a pony! Hands up everyone who knows what a baby horse is.'

All the right arms in the room, except James's and Miss Smith's, shot upwards. Miss Smith smiled at James.

'Everyone knows,' she said. 'Everyone knows what a baby horse is called except James.'

James thought: I'll run away. I'll join the tinkers and live in a tent.

'What's a baby horse called?' Miss Smith asked the class and the class shouted:

'Foal, Miss Smith.'

'A foal, James,' Miss Smith repeated. 'A baby horse is a foal, James dear.'

I knew Miss Smith. I knew but—'

Miss Smith laughed and the class laughed, and afterwards nobody would play with James because he was so silly to think that a baby horse was a pony.

James was an optimist about Miss Smith. He thought it might be different when the class went on the summer picnic or sat tightly together at the Christmas party, eating cake and biscuits and having their mugs filled from big enamel jugs. But it never was different. James got left behind when everyone was racing across the fields at the picnic and Miss Smith had to wait impatiently, telling the class that James would have to have his legs stretched. And at the party she heaped his plate with seed-cake because she imagined, so she said, that he was the kind of child who enjoyed such fare.

Once James found himself alone with Miss Smith in the class-room. She was sitting at her desk correcting some home-work. James was staring in front of him, admiring a fountain pen that the day before his mother had bought for him. It was a small fountain pen, coloured purple and black and white. James believed it to be elegant.

It was very quiet in the class-room. Soundlessly Miss Smith's red pencil ticked and crossed and underlined. Without looking up, she said: 'Why don't you go out and play?'

'Yes, Miss Smith,' said James. He walked to the door, clipping his pen into his pocket. As he turned the handle he heard Miss Smith utter a sound of irritation. He turned and saw that the point of her pencil had broken. 'Miss Smith, you may borrow my pen. You can fill it with red ink. It's quite a good pen.'

James crossed the room and held out his pen. Miss Smith unscrewed the cap and prodded at the paper with the nib. 'What a funny pen, James!' she said. 'Look it can't write.'

'There's no ink in it,' James explained. 'You've got to fill it with red ink, Miss Smith.'

But Miss Smith smiled and handed the pen back. 'What a silly boy you are to waste your money on such a poor pen!'

'But I didn't —'

'Come along now, James, aren't you going to lend me your pencil-sharpener?'

'I haven't got a pencil-sharpener, Miss Smith.'

'No pencil-sharpener? Oh James, James, you haven't got anything, have you?'

When Miss Smith married she stopped teaching, and

James imagined he had escaped her for ever. But the town they lived in was a small one and they often met in the street or in a shop. And Miss Smith, who at first found marriage rather boring, visited the school quite regularly. 'How's James?' she would say, smiling alarmingly at him. 'How's my droopy, old James?'

When Miss Smith had been married for about a year she gave birth to a son, which occupied her a bit. He was a fine child, eight pounds six ounces, with a good long head and blue eyes. Miss Smith was delighted with him, and her husband, a solicitor, complimented her sweetly and bought cigars and drinks for all his friends. In time, mother and son were seen daily taking the air: Miss Smith on her trim little legs and the baby in his frilly pram. James, meeting the two, said: 'Miss Smith, may I see the baby?' But Miss Smith laughed and said that she was not Miss Smith any more. She wheeled the pram rapidly away, as though the child within it might be affected by the proximity of the other.

'What a dreadful little boy that James Machen is,' Miss Smith reported to her husband. 'I feel so sorry for the parents.'

'Do I know him? What does the child look like?'

'Small, dear, like a weasel wearing glasses. He quite gives me the creeps.'

Almost without knowing it, James developed a compulsion about Miss Smith. At first it was quite a simple compulsion: just that James had to talk to God about Miss Smith every night before he went to sleep, and try to find out from God what it was about him that Miss Smith so despised. Every night he lay in bed and had his conversation, and if once he forgot it James knew that the next time he met Miss Smith she would probably say something that might make him drop down dead.

After about a month of conversation with God James discovered he had found the solution. It was so simple that he marvelled he had never thought of it before. He began to get up very early in the morning and pick bunches of flowers. He would carry them down the street to Miss Smith's house and place them on a window-sill. He was careful not to be seen, by Miss Smith or by anyone else. He knew that if anyone saw him the plan couldn't work. When he had picked all the flowers in his own garden he started to pick them from other people's gardens. He became rather clever at moving silently through the gardens, picking flowers for Miss Smith.

Unfortunately, though, on the day that James carried his thirty-first bunch of blooms to the house of Miss Smith he was observed. He saw the curtains move as he reached up to lay the flowers on the window-sill. A moment later Miss Smith, in her dressing-gown, had caught him by the shoulder and pulled him into the house.

'James Machen! It would be James Machen, wouldn't it? Flowers from the creature, if you please! What are you up to, you dozy James?'

James said nothing. He looked at Miss Smith's dressing-gown and thought it was particularly pretty: blue and woolly, with an edging of silk.

'You've been trying to get us into trouble,' cried Miss Smith. 'You've been stealing flowers all over the town and putting them at our house. You're an underhand child, James.'

James stared at her and then ran away.

After that, James thought of Miss Smith almost all the time. He thought of her face when she had caught him with the flowers, and how she had afterwards told his father and nearly everyone else in the town. He thought of how his father had had to say he was sorry to Miss Smith, and how his mother and father had quarrelled about the affair. He counted up all the things Miss Smith had ever said to him, and all the things she had ever done to him, like giving him seed-cake at the Christmas party. He hadn't meant to harm Miss Smith as she said he had. Giving people flowers wasn't unkind; it was to show them you liked them and wanted them to like you.

'When somebody hurts you,' James said to the man who

138

came to cut the grass, 'what do you do about it?'

'Well,' said the man, 'I suppose you hurt them back.'

'Supposing you can't,' James argued.

'Oh, but you always can. It's easy to hurt people.'

'It's not, really,' James said.

'Look,' said the man, 'all I've got to do is reach out and give you a clip on the ear. That'd hurt you.'

'But I couldn't do that to you because you're so big. How d'you hurt someone who's bigger than you?'

'It's easier to hurt people who are weaker. People who are weaker are always the ones who get hurt.'

'Can't you hurt someone who is stronger?'

The grass-cutter thought for a time. 'You have to be cunning to do that. You've got to find the weak spot. Everyone has a weak spot.'

'Have you got a weak spot?'

'I suppose so.'

'Could I hurt you on your weak spot?'

'You don't want to hurt me, James.'

'No, but just could I?'

'Yes, I suppose you could.'

'Well then?'

'My little daughter's smaller than you. If you hurt her, you see, you'd be hurting me. It'd be the same, you see.'

'I see,' said James.

All was not well with Miss Smith. Life, which had been so happy when her baby was born, seemed now to be directed against her. Perhaps it was that the child was becoming difficult, going through a teething phase that was pleasant for no one; or perhaps it was that Miss Smith recognised in him some trait she disliked and knew that she would be obliged to watch it develop, powerless to intervene. Whatever the reason, she felt depressed. She often thought of her teaching days, of the big square schoolroom with the children's models on the shelves and the pictures of kings on the walls. Nostalgically, she recalled the feel of frosty air on her face as she rode her bicycle through the town, her mind already practising the first lesson of the day. She had loved those winter days: the children stamping their feet in the playground, the stove groaning and crackling, so red and so fierce that it had to be penned off for safety's sake. It had been good to feel tired, good to bicycle home, shopping a bit on the way, home to tea and the wireless and an evening of reading by the fire. It wasn't that she regretted anything; it was just that now and again, for a day or two, she felt she would like to return to the past.

'My dear,' Miss Smith's husband said, 'you really will have to be more careful.'

'But I am. Truly I am. I'm just as careful as anyone can be.'

'Of course you are. But it's a difficult age. Perhaps, you know, you need a holiday.'

'But I've had difficult ages to deal with for years —'

'Now now, my dear, it's not quite the same, teaching a class of kids.'

'But it shouldn't be as difficult. I don't know —'

'You're tired. Tied to a child all day long, every day of the week, it's no joke. We'll take an early holiday.'

Miss Smith did feel tired, but she knew that it wasn't tiredness that was really the trouble. Her baby was almost three, and for two years she knew she had been making mistakes with him. Yet somehow she felt that they weren't her mistakes: it was as though some other person occasionally possessed her; a negligent, worthless kind of person who was cruel, almost criminal, in her carelessness. Once she had discovered the child crawling on the pavement beside his pram: she had forgotten apparently to attach his harness to the pram hooks. Once there had been beads in his pram, hundreds of them, small and red and made of glass. A woman had drawn her attention to the danger, regarding curiously the supplier of so unsuitable a plaything. 'In his nose he was putting one, dear. And may have swallowed a dozen already. It could kill a mite, you know.' The beads were hers, but how the child had got them she could not fathom. Earlier, when he had been only a couple of month, she had come into his nursery to find an excited cat scratching at the clothes of his cot; and on another occasion she had found him eating a turnip. She wondered if she might be suffering from some kind of serious absent-mindedness, or blackouts. Her doctor told her, uncomfortably, that she was a little run down.

'I'm a bad mother,' said Miss Smith to herself; and she cried as she looked at her child, warm and pretty in his sleep.

But her carelessness continued and people remarked that it was funny in a teacher. Her husband was upset and unhappy, and finally suggested that they should employ someone to look after the child. 'Someone else?' said Miss Smith. 'Someone *else*? Am I then incapable? Am I so wretched and stupid that I cannot look after my own child? You speak to me as though I were half crazy.' She felt confused and sick and miserable. The marriage teetered beneath the tension, and there was no question of further children.

Then there were two months without incident. Miss Smith began to feel better; she was getting the hang of things; once again she was in control of her daily life. Her child grew and flourished. He trotted nimbly beside her, he spoke his own language, he was wayward and irresponsible, and to Miss Smith and her husband he was intelligent and full of charm. Every day Miss Smith saved up the sayings and doings of this child and duly reported them to her husband. 'He is quite intrepid,' Miss Smith said, and she told her husband how the child would tumble about the room, trying to stand on his head. 'He has an aptitude for athletics,' her husband remarked. They laughed that they, so unathletic in their ways, should have produced so physically lively an offspring.

'And how has our little monster been today?' Miss Smith's husband asked, entering the house one evening at his usual time.

Miss Smith smiled, happy after a good, quiet day. 'Like gold,' she said.

Her husband smiled too, glad that the child had not been a nuisance to her and glad that his son, for his own sake, was capable of adequate behaviour. 'I'll just take a peep at him,' he announced, and he ambled off to the nursery.

He sighed with relief as he climbed the stairs, thankful that all was once again well in the house. He was still sighing when he opened the nursery door and smelt gas. It hissed insidiously from the unlit fire. The room was sweet with it. The child, sleeping, sucked it into his lungs.

The child's face was blue. They carried him from the room, both of them helpless and inadequate in the situation. And then they waited, without speaking, while his life was recovered, until the moment when the doctor, white-coated and stern, explained that it had been a nearer thing than he would wish again to handle.

'This is too serious,' Miss Smith's husband said. 'We cannot continue like this. Something must be done.'

'I cannot understand —'

'It happens too often. The strain is too much for me, dear.'

'I cannot understand it.'

Every precaution had been taken with the gas-fire in the nursery. The knob that controlled the gas pressure was a key and the key was removable. Certainly, the control point was within the child's reach but one turned it on or off, slipped the key out of its socket and placed it on the mantelpiece. That was the simple rule.

'You forgot to take out the key,' Miss Smith's husband said. In his mind an idea took on a shape that frightened him. He shied away, watching it advance, knowing that he possessed neither the emotional nor mental equipment to fight it.

'No, no, no,' Miss Smith said. 'I never forget it. I turned the fire off and put the key on the mantelpiece. I remember distinctly.'

He stared at her, drilling his eyes into hers, hopelessly seeking the truth. When he spoke his voice was dry and weary.

'The facts speak for themselves. You cannot suggest there's another solution?'

'But it's absurd. It means he got out of his cot, turned the key, returned to bed and went to sleep.'

'Or that you turned off the fire and idly turned it on again.'

'I couldn't have; how could I?'

Miss Smith's husband didn't know. His imagination, like a pair of calipers, grasped the ugly thought and held it before him. The facts were on its side, he could not ignore them: his wife was deranged in her mind. Consciously or otherwise she was trying to kill their child.

'The window,' Miss Smith said. 'It was open when I left it. It always is, for air. Yet you found it closed.'

'The child certainly could not have done that. I cannot see what you are suggesting.'

'I don't know. I don't know what I am suggesting. Except that I don't understand.'

'He is too much for you, dear, and that's all there is to it. You must have help.'

'We can't afford it.'

'Be that as it may, we must. We have the child to think of, if not ourselves.'

'But one child! One child cannot be too much for anyone. Look, I'll be extra careful in future. After all, it is the first thing like this that has happened for ages.'

'I'm sorry, dear. We must advertise for a woman.'

'Please —'

'Darling, I'm sorry. It's no use talking. We have talked enough and it has got us nowhere. This is something to be sensible about.'

'Please let's try again.'

'And in the meanwhile? In the meanwhile our child's life must be casually risked day in, day out?'

'No, no.'

Miss Smith pleaded, but her husband said nothing further. He pulled hard on his pipe, biting it between his jaws, unhappy and confused in his mind.

Miss Smith's husband did indeed advertise for a woman to see to the needs of their child, but it was, in fact, unnecessary in the long run to employ her. Because on his third birthday, late in the afternoon, the child disappeared. Miss Smith had put him in the garden. It was a perfectly safe garden: he played there often. Yet when she called him for his tea he did not come; and when she looked for the reason she found that he was not there. The small gate that led to the fields at the back of the house was open. She had not opened it; she rarely used it. Distractedly, she thought he must have managed to release the catch himself. 'That is quite impossible,' her husband said. 'It's too high and too stiff.' He looked at her oddly, confirmed in his mind that she wished to be rid of her child. Together they tramped the fields with the police, but although they covered a great area and were out for most of the night they were unsuccessful.

When the search continued in the light of the morning it was a search without hope, and the hopelessness in time turned into the fear of what discovery would reveal. 'We must accept the facts.' Miss Smith's husband said, but she alone continued to hope. She dragged her legs over the wide countryside, seeking a miracle but finding neither trace nor word of her child's wanderings.

A small boy, so quiet she scarcely noticed him, stopped her once by a sawmill. He spoke some shy salutation, and when she blinked her eyes at his face she saw that he was James Machen. She passed him by, thinking only that she envied him his life, that for him to live and her child to die was proof indeed of a mocking Providence. She prayed to this Providence, promising a score of resolutions if only all would be well.

But nothing was well, and Miss Smith brooded on the thought that her husband had not voiced. *I released the gate*

*myself. For some reason I have not wanted this child. God knows
I loved him, and surely it wasn't too weak a love? Is it that I've
loved so many other children that I have none left that is real
enough for my own?* Pathetic, baseless, theories flooded into
Miss Smith's mind. Her thoughts floundered and collapsed
into wretched chaos.

'Miss Smith,' James said, 'would you like to see your
baby?'

He stood at her kitchen door, and Miss Smith, hearing
the words, was incapable immediately of grasping their
meaning. The sun, reflected in the kitchen, was mirrored
again in the child's glasses. He smiled at her, more con-
fidently than she remembered, revealing a silvery wire
stretched across his teeth.

'What did you say?' Miss Smith asked.

'I said, would you like to see your baby?'

Miss Smith had not slept for a long time. She was afraid
to sleep because of the nightmares. Her hair hung lank
about her shoulders, her eyes were dead and seemed to
have fallen back deeper into her skull. She stood listening
to this child, nodding her head up and down, very slowly,
in a mechanical way. Her left hand moved gently back and
forth on the smooth surface of her kitchen table.

'My baby?' Miss Smith said. 'My baby?'

'You have lost your baby,' James reminded her.

Miss Smith nodded a little faster.

'I will show you,' James said.

He caught her hand and led her from the house, through
the garden and through the gate into the fields. Hand in
hand they walked through the grass, over the canal bridge
and across the warm, ripe meadows.

'I will pick you flowers,' James said and he ran to gather
poppies and cowparsley and blue, beautiful corn-flowers.

'You give people flowers,' James said, 'because you like
them and you want them to like you.'

She carried the flowers and James skipped and danced
beside her, hurrying her along. She heard him laughing,

145

she looked at him and saw his small weasel face twisted into a merriment that frightened her.

The sun was fierce on Miss Smith's neck and shoulders. Sweat gathered on her forehead and ran down her cheeks. She felt it on her body, tightening her clothes to her back and thighs. Only the child's hand was cool, and beneath her fingers she assessed its strength, wondering about its history. Again the child laughed.

On the heavy air his laughter rose and fell; it quivered through his body and twitched lightly in his hand. It came as a giggle, then a breathless spasm; it rose like a storm from him; it rippled to gentleness; and it pounded again like the firing of guns in her ear. It would not stop. She knew it would not stop. As they walked together on this summer's day the laughter would continue until they arrived at the horror, until the horror was complete.

The Forty-seventh Saturday

Mavie awoke and remembered at once that it was Saturday. She lay for a while, alone with that thought, considering it and relishing it. Then she thought of details: the ingredients of a lunch, the cleaning of the kitchen floor, the tidying of her bedroom. She rose and reached for her dressing-gown. In the kitchen she found a small pad of paper and wrote in pencil these words: *mackerel, parmesan cheese, garlic.* Then she drew back the curtains, placed a filled kettle over a gas jet and shook cornflakes on to a plate.

Some hours later, about mid-day, Mr. McCarthy stood thoughtfully in a wine-shop. He sighed and then said:

Vin rosé. The larger size. Is it a litre? I don't know what it's called.'

'Jumbo *vin rosé,*' the assistant murmured, ignoring the demands of the accented word. 'Fourteen and seven.'

It was not a wine-shop in which Mr. McCarthy had ever before made a purchase. He paused, his hand inside his jacket, the tips of his fingers touching the leather of his wallet.

'Fourteen and seven?'

The assistant, perceiving clearly that Mr. McCarthy had arrested the action with which he had planned to draw money from within his clothes, took no notice. He blew on the glass of the bottle because the bottle was dusty. Whistling thickly with tongue and lips, he tore a piece of brown paper and proceeded to wrap with it. He placed the parcel in a carrier bag.

'I thought it was ten shillings that size,' Mr. McCarthy said. 'I have got it in another place for ten shillings.'

The assistant stared at him, incredulous.

'I buy a lot of *vin rosé*,' Mr McCarthy explained.

The assistant, a man of thirty-five with a face that was pock-marked, spoke no word but stared on. In his mind he was already retailing the incident to his superior when, an hour or so later, that person should return. He scrutinised Mr. McCarthy, so that when the time came he might lend authority to his tale with an accurate description of the man who had demanded *vin rosé* and then had argued about the charged price. He saw before him a middle-aged man of medium height, with a hat and spectacles and a moustache.

'Well, I haven't time to argue,' Mr. McCarthy handed the man a pound note and received his change. 'Three pence short, that is,' he said, and the assistant explained:

'The carrier bag. It's necessary nowadays to charge. You understand?'

But Mr. McCarthy lifted the wine out of the bag, saying that the brown paper wrapping was quite sufficient, and the assistant handed him a threepenny piece.

'I take a taxi,' Mr. McCarthy explained. 'It's no hardship to carry.'

In the flat Mavie laid two mackerel on the smoking fat of the frying-pan and sniffed the air. A plastic apron covered her navy-blue, rather old-fashioned suit. Her fair hair, recently released from curling-pins, quivered splendidly about her head; her bosom heaved as she drew the tasty air into her lungs. She walked from the stove to the kitchen table, seeking a glass of medium dry sherry that a minute or two previously she had poured and placed somewhere.

'Ta-ra-ta-ta-ta-ta-ta-ta, ta-ta-ta-ta-ta-ta,' tuned Mr. McCarthy in his taxi-cab, trying to put from his mind the extra four and sevenpence that he had been obliged to spend on the wine. 'A basement place,' he called to the driver. 'You'll know it by a motor-cycle and side-car parked outside.' The driver made no response.

'Motor-bike and side-car,' repeated Mr. McCarthy.

'Parked by a lamp-post, number twenty-one. D'you understand?'

'Twenty-one, Roeway Road,' said the driver. 'We'll endeavour.'

Mr. McCarthy closed his eyes and stretched his legs stiffly in front of him. He thought of Mavie, as was suitable at that moment. He saw her standing by the edge of the kitchen table, with a cigarette protruding from the left-hand extremity of her mouth and the thumb and forefinger of her right hand grasping a glass which contained sherry and which bore, painted around it on the outside, two thin lines, one in red, the other in gold. It was the forty-seventh time that Mr. McCarthy had made this mid-day journey, in a taxi-cab with a bottle of wine.

'Doesn't he want you to dress up? the girls had asked when first she had told them. 'Pith helmets, chukka boots?' Mavie had found that funny. She had laughed and said: 'Dress up? Rather the opposite!' But that was at the very beginning of the affair, before she had fallen so deeply in love with him.

'Hullo,' Mavie, holding the sherry glass before her, struck a pose in the basement kitchen. She had taken off her plastic apron.

'Hullo, Mavie.' He held out the bottle, his hat still upon his head, his soft raincoat creased and seeming unclean. 'I've brought some wine. A little wine. I thought it would cheer us up.' He had let himself in, for the door was always on the latch. He had clicked the Yale catch behind him, as he had long since learned she liked him to do, so that no disturbances might later take place. 'I don't care for disturbances,' Mavie had said on the fifth occasion: an embarrassing time, when a coal-heaver, mistaking the basement for the basement next door, had walked into her bedroom with a sack on his back to find Mr. McCarthy and herself playing about on the covers of her bed.

'My, my, you're looking sweet.' He removed his hat and overcoat and cast his eye about for a corkscrew. It was his policy on these visits to prime himself beforehand with

149

two measures of brandy and, having made his entry, to take an immediate glass of *vin rosé*. He did not care for Mavie's sherry. *British sherry* was how the label described it; a qualification that put Mr. McCarthy off.

'I love that costume.' He had said this before, referring to Mavie's navy-blue coat and skirt. In reply she had once or twice pointed out that it had been, originally, the property of her sister Linda.

Mr. McCarthy could smell the fish. He could sense the atmosphere rich with mackerel and the perfumed mist with which Mavie had sprayed the room.

'I'm doing a nice fresh mackerel in a custard sauce,' Mavie announced, moving towards the stove. She had been closely embraced by Mr. McCarthy, who was now a little shaken, caught between the promise of the embrace and the thought of mackerel in a sauce. He imagined he must have heard incorrectly: he could not believe that the sauce was a custard one. 'Custard!' he said. 'Custard?'

Mavie stirred the contents of a bowl. She remembered the first time: she had made an omlette; the mushrooms with which she had filled it had not cooked properly and Mr. McCarthy had remarked upon the fact. She could have wept, watching him move the mushrooms to the side of his plate. 'Have them on toast,' she had cried. 'I'll cook them a bit more, love, and you can have them on a nice piece of toast.' But he had shaken his head, and then, to show that all was well, he had taken her into his arms and had at once begun to unzip her skirt.

'Custard?' said Mr. McCarthy again, aware of some revulsion in his bowels.

'A garlic custard sauce. I read it in that column.'

'My dear, I'd as soon have a lightly boiled egg. This wretched old trouble again.'

'Oh, you poor thing. But fish is as easy to digest. A small helping. I'd have steamed had I known. You poor soul. Sit down, for heaven's sake.'

He was thinking that he would vomit if he had to lift a single forkful of mackerel and garlic custard sauce to his

150

lips. He would feel a retching at the back of his throat and before another second passed there would be an accident.

'Love, I should have told you: I am off fish in any shape or form. The latest thing, I am on a diet of soft-boiled eggs. I'm a terrible trouble to you, Mavie love.'

She came to where he was sitting, drinking his way through the wine, and kissed him. She said not to worry about anything.

Mr. McCarthy had told Mavie more lies than he had ever told anyone else. He had invented trouble with his stomach so that he could insist upon simple food, even though Mavie, forgetfully or hopefully, always cooked more elaborately. He had invented a Saturday appointment at four o'clock every week so that no dawdling would be required of him after he had exacted what he had come to look upon as his due. He had invented a wife and two children so that Mavie might not get ideas above her station.

'Brush your teeth, Mavie, like a good girl.' Mr. McCarthy was being practical, fearful of the garlic. He spoke with confidence, knowing that Mavie would see it as reasonable that she should brush her teeth before the moments of love.

While she was in the bathroom he hummed a tune and reflected on his continuing good fortune. He drank more wine and when Mavie returned bade her drink some, too. It could only happen on Saturdays because the girl whom Mavie shared the flat with, Eithne, went away for the week-ends.

'Well, this is pleasant,' said Mr. McCarthy, sitting her on his knee, stroking her navy-blue clothes. She sat there, a little heavy for him, swinging her legs until her shoes slipped off.

This Saturday was Mavie's birthday. Today she was twenty-seven, while Mr. McCarthy remained at fifty-two. She had, the night before and for several other nights and days, considered the fact, wondering whether or not to make anything of it, wondering whether or not to let Mr.

McCarthy know. She had thought, the Saturday before, that it might seem a little pushing to say that it was her birthday in a week; it might seem that her words contained the suggestion that Mr. McCarthy should arm himself with a present or should contrive to transform the day into a special occasion. She thought ecstatically of his arriving at the house with a wrapped box and sitting down and saying: 'What lovely mackerel!' and putting it to her then that since this was her twenty-seventh birthday he would arrange to spend the whole afternoon and the night as well. 'We shall take to the West End later on,' Mr. McCarthy had said in Mavie's mind, 'and shall go to a show, that thing at the Palladium. I have the tickets in my wallet.'

'What terrible old weather it is,' said Mr. McCarthy. 'You wouldn't know whether you're coming or going.'

Mavie made a noise of agreement. She remembered other birthdays: a year she had been given a kite, the time that her cake, its flavour chosen by her, had not succeeded in the oven and had come to the table lumpy and grey, disguised with hundreds and thousands. She had cried, and her mother had picked up a teaspoon and rapped her knuckles. 'After the show,' said Mr. McCarthy, 'what about a spot of dinner in a little place I've heard of? And then liqueurs before we return in style to your little nest.' As he spoke Mr. McCarthy nuzzled her neck, and Mavie realised that he was, in fact, nuzzling her neck, though he was not speaking.

'Today is a special day,' said Mavie. 'It's a very special November day.'

Mr. McCarthy laughed. 'Every Saturday is a special day for me. Every Saturday is outlined in red on my heart.' And he initiated some horseplay which prevented Mavie from explaining.

Born beneath the sign of Scorpio, she was meant to be strong, fearless and enterprising. As a child she had often been in trouble, not because of naughtiness but because she had been dreamy about her work. She dreamed now, dominated by an image of Mr. McCarthy rushing out of a sudden for flowers. She saw him returning, blooms everywhere, saying he had telephoned to put off his Saturday appointment and had telephoned his home to say that he had been called away on vital business. She felt his hands seeking the outline of her ribs, a thing he liked to do. They lay in silence for a while, and increasingly she felt low and sad.

'How lovely you are,' murmured Mr. McCarthy. 'Oh, Mavie, Mavie.'

She squeezed the length of pale flesh that was Mr. McCarthy's arm. She thought suddenly of the day the coalheaver had arrived and felt her neck going red at the memory. She remembered the first day, rolling down her stockings and seeing her lover watching her, he already naked, standing still and seeming puzzled, near the electric fire. She had not been a virgin that day, but in the meanwhile she had not once been unfaithful to him.

'Tell me you love me,' Mavie cried, forgetting about her birthday, abruptly caught up in a new emotion. 'Tell me now; it worries me sometimes.'

'Of course it does. Of course I do. I'm all for you, Mavie, as I've said a thousand times.'

'It's not that I doubt you, honey, only sometimes between one Saturday and another I feel a depression. It's impossible to say. I mean, it's hard to put into words. Have you got a fag?'

Mr. McCarthy shook his head on the pillow. She knew he did not smoke: why then did she ask? It was like the custard sauce all over again. When he went to the trouble of inventing stomach trouble, you'd think she'd take the trouble to remember it.

'You don't smoke. I always ask and you always don't say anything and I always remember then. Am I very irritating to you, honey? Tell me you love me. Tell me I'm not irritating to you.'

'Mavie.'

'You don't like me today. I feel it. Jesus, I'm sorry about

153

the mackerel. Tell the truth now, you don't like me to-day.'

'Oh yes, I do. I love you. I love you.'

'You don't like me.' She spoke as though she had not heard his protestations; she spaced the words carefully, giving the same emphasis to each.

'I love you,' said Mr. McCarthy. 'Indeed I do.'

She shook her head, and rose and walked to the kitchen, where she found cigarettes and matches.

'My Mavie,' said Mr. McCarthy from the bed, assuring himself that he was not finished yet, that he had not fully exacted his pleasurable due. 'Mavie, my young heart,' he murmured, and he began to laugh, thinking that merriment in the atmosphere would cheer matters up. 'Shall I do a little dance for you?'

Mavie, cigarette aglow, pulled the sheets around her as Mr. McCarthy vacated the bed and stood, his arms outstretched, on the centre of the floor. He began to dance, as on many occasions, before he had danced, swaying about without much tempo. When first he performed in this way for her he had explained that his dance was an expression of his passion, representing, so he said, roses and presents of jewellery and lamé gowns. Once Mr. McCarthy had asked Mavie to take the braces off his trousers and strike him with them while he acted out his dance. He was guilty, he said, because in their life together there was neither roses nor jewels nor restaurant dinners. But Mavie, shocked that he should feel like that, had refused his request, saying there was no cause for punishment. Sulkily, he had maintained otherwise, though he had not ever again suggested chastisement.

'How's that?' said Mr. McCarthy, ending with a gesture. Mavie said nothing. She threw back the bed-clothes and Mr. McCarthy strode jauntily towards her, a smile shaping beneath his moustache.

'I often wonder about her,' Mavie said a moment later. 'It's only natural. You can't help that.'

Mr. McCarthy said: 'My wife's a hard case. She's well

able to take care of herself. I'm on a leash where the wife is concerned.'

'I don't even know her name.'

'Oh, Mavie, Mavie. Isn't Mrs. McCarthy enough?'

'I'm jealous. I'm sorry, honey.'

'No bother, Mavie. No bother, love.'

'I see her as a black-haired woman. Tall and sturdy. Would you rather we didn't speak of her?'

'It would be easier, certainly.'

'I'm sorry, honey.'

'No bother.'

'It's only jealousy. The green-eyed monster.'

'No need to be jealous, Mavie. No need at all. There's no love lost between Mrs. McCarthy and myself. We never go together nowadays.'

'What sign is she under?'

'Sign, love?'

'Sagittarius? Leo? When's her birthday?'

Mr. McCarthy's small eyes screwed up.

He looked through the lashes. He said:

'The twenty-ninth of March.'

'You make an occasion of it, do you? In the home, with the children around? You all give her presents, I suppose. Is there a special cake?'

'The wife likes a jam-roll. She buys one at Lyons.'

'And the children get her little gifts? Things from Woolworth's?'

'Something like that.'

'When I was little I used to buy presents in Woolworth's. My dad used to take my by the hand. I suppose you did, too. And your wife.'

'Yes, love, I suppose so.'

'I often think of your wife. I can't help it. I see her in my mind's eye.'

'She's a big woman,' said Mr. McCarthy meditatively. 'Bigger than you, Mavie. A big, dark woman — more than that I won't say.'

'Oh, honey, I never meant to pry.'

'It's not prying I mind, Mavie. No, you're not prying. It's just that I don't wish to soil the hour.'

When Mr. McCarthy had said that, he heard the words echoing in his mind as words occasionally do. *I don't wish to soil the hour.* Mavie was silent, feeling the words to be beautiful. *I don't wish to soil the hour,* she thought. She drew her finger-nails along the taut skin of Mr. McCarthy's thigh. 'Oh God,' said Mr. McCarthy.

She knew that when he left, at twenty to four, she would sit alone in her dressing-gown and weep. She would wash the dirty dishes from lunch and she would wash his lovingly: she would wash and dry his egg-cup and be aware that it was his. She knew that that was absurd, but she knew that it would happen because it had happened before. She did not think it odd, as Mr. McCarthy had often thought, that she, so pretty and still young, should love so passionately a man of fifty-two. She adored every shred of him; she longed for his presence and the touch of his hand. 'Oh, my honey, my honey,' cried Mavie, throwing her body on the body of Mr. McCarthy and wrapping him up in her plump limbs.

At half-past three Mr. McCarthy, who had dropped into a light doze, woke to the awareness of a parched throat and a desire for tea. He sighed and caressed the fair hair that lay on the pillow beside him.

'I'll make a cup of tea,' said Mavie.

'*Merci,*' whispered Mr. McCarthy.

They drank tea in the kitchen while Mr. McCarthy buttoned his waistcoat and drew on his socks. 'I've bought a bow tie,' he confided, 'though I'm still a little shy in it. Maybe next week I'll try it out on you.'

'You could ask me anything under the sun and I'd do it for you. You could ask me anything, I love you that much.'

Hearing this, Mr. McCarthy paused in the lacing of a boot. He thought of his braces, taut now about his shoulders; he thought of a foot fetish he had read about in the public library.

'I love you that much,' whispered Mavie.

'And I you,' said Mr. McCarthy.

'I dream of you at nights.'

'I dream of you, my dear.'

Mavie sighed and looked over her shoulder, ill at ease. 'I cannot think of you dreaming of me.'

'I dream of you in my narrow twin bed, with the dark-haired woman in the twin beside it.'

'Don't speak like that. Don't talk to me of the bedroom.'

'I'm sorry.'

'I can't bear the thought of the twin beds in that room. I've told you before, honey.'

'Oh, Mavie, Mavie, if we could be together.'

'I love you that much.'

For a moment there was silence in the kitchen. Then, having tilted his cup to drain it of tea, Mr. McCarthy rose to go.

As he crossed the floor his eyes fell on a birthday card propped up on the mantelshelf. It registered with him at once that the day was Mavie's birthday, and for a moment he considered remarking on that fact. Then he remembered the time and he kissed her on the head, his usual form of farewell. 'The forty-seventh time,' he murmured. 'Today was the forty-seventh.'

She walked with him along the passage to the door of the flat. She watched him mount the basement steps and watched his legs move briskly by the railings above. His footsteps died away and she returned to the kitchen and poured herself a cup of tea. She thought of him keeping his Saturday appointment, a business appointment he had always called it, and afterwards returning on a bus to his suburb. She saw him entering a door, opening it with a latchkey, being greeted by a dog and two children and the big, dark woman who was his wife. The dog barked loudly and the woman shrilled abuse, upbraiding her husband for a misdemeanour or some piece of forgetfulness or some small deceit discovered. She could feel his tiredness as he stood in his own hall, the latchkey still poised between his fingers, like a man at bay. Her eyes closed as she held that image in her mind; tears slipped from beneath their lids.

The bus let Mr. McCarthy down at an Odeon cinema. He moved rapidly, checking his watch against a brightly lit clock that hung out over a shop. He was reckoning as he walked that there was time to have another cup of tea, with a Danish pastry perhaps, because he felt quite peckish. Afterwards, as always on a Saturday, he'd go to the pictures.

Mr. McNamara

'How was he?' my mother asked on the morning of my thirteenth birthday.

She spoke while pouring tea into my father's extra-large breakfast cup, the last remaining piece of a flowered set, *Ville de Lyon* clematis on a leafy ground. My father had a special knife and fork as well, the knife another relic of the past, the fork more ordinary, extra-strong because my father was always breaking forks.

'Oh, he's well enough,' he said on the morning of my thirteenth birthday, while I sat patiently. 'The old aunt's licking us again.'

My mother, passing him his tea, nodded. She remarked that in her opinion Mr. McNamara's aunt should be placed in an asylum, which was what she always said when the subject of Mr. McNamara's aunt, reputedly alcoholic, cropped up.

My mother was tallish and slender, but softly so. There was nothing sharp or angular about my mother, nothing wiry or hard. She had fair hair and rather misty blue eyes, and she seemed always to be on the point of smiling. My father, in contrast, was bulky, a man with a brown face and a brown forehead stretching back where hair once had been, with heavy brown-backed hands and eyes the same shade of blue mist as my mother's. They were gentle with one another in a way that was similar also, and when they disagreed or argued their voices weren't ever raised. They could be angry with us, but not with one another. They meted out punishments for us jointly, sharing disapproval or disappointment. We felt doubly ashamed when our

159

misdemeanours were uncovered.

'The train was like a Frigidaire,' my father said. 'Two hours late at the halt. Poor Flannagan nearly had pneumonia waiting.' The whole country had ivy growing over it, he said, like ivy on a gravestone. Eating bacon and sausages with his special knife and fork, he nodded in agreement with himself. 'Ivy-clad Ireland,' he said when his mouth was momentarily empty of food. 'Anthracite motor-cars, refrigerators on the Great Southern Railway. Another thing, Molly: it's the opinion in Dublin that six months' time will see foreign soldiers parading themselves on O'Connell Street. German or English, take your pick, and there's damn all Dev can do about it.'

My mother smiled at him and sighed. Then, as though to cheer us all up, my father told a story that Mr. McNamara had told him, about a coal merchant whom Mr. Mc-Namara had apparently known in his youth. The story had to do with the ill-fitting nature of the coal merchant's artificial teeth and the loss of the teeth when he'd once been swimming at Ringsend. Whenever my father returned from a meeting with Mr. McNamara he brought us back such stories, as well as the current opinion of Mr. Mc-Namara on the state of the nation and the likelihood of the nation becoming involved in the war. 'The opinion in Dublin' was the opinion of Mr. McNamara, as we all knew. Mr. McNamara drove a motor-car powered by gas because there wasn't much petrol to be had. The gas, so my father said, was manufactured by anthracite in a burner stuck on to the back of Mr. McNamara's Ford V-8.

Returning each time from Dublin, my father bore messages and gifts from Mr. McNamara, a tin of Jacob's biscuits or bars of chocolate. He was a man who'd never married and who lived on inherited means, in a house in Palmerston Road, with members of his family – the elderly alcoholic aunt who should have been in an asylum, a sister and a brother-in-law. The sister, now Mrs. Matchette, had earlier had theatrical ambitions, but her husband, employed in the National Bank, had persuaded her away from them. My father had never actually met Mr. Mc-Namara's insane aunt or Mrs. Matchette or her husband: they lived through Mr. McNamara for him, at second hand, and for us they lived through my father, at a further remove. We had a vivid image of all of them, Mrs. Matchette thin as a blade of grass, endlessly smoking and playing patience, her husband small and solemn, neatly moustached, with dark neat hair combed straight back from what Mr. McNamara had called a 'squashed forehead'. Mr. McNamara himself we imagined as something of a presence: prematurely white-haired, portly, ponderous in speech and motion. Mr. McNamara used to frequent the bar of a hotel called Fleming's, an old-fashioned place where you could get snuff as well as tobacco, and tea, coffee and Bovril as well as alcoholic drinks. It was here that my father met him on his visits to Dublin. It was a comfort to go there, my father said, when his business for the day was done, and sit in a leather chair and listen to the chit-chat of his old companion. The bar would fill with smoke from their Sweet Afton cigarettes, while my father listened to the latest about the people in the house in Palmerston Road, and the dog they had, a spaniel called Wolfe Tone, and a maid called Trixie O'Shea, from Skibbereen. There was a ritual about it, my father smoking and listening, just as a day or so later he'd smoke and we'd listen ourselves, at breakfast-time in our house in the country.

There were my three sisters and myself: I was the oldest, the only boy. We lived in a house that had been in the family for several generations, three miles from Curransbridge, where the Dublin train halted if anyone wanted it to, and where my father's granary and mill were. Because of the shortage of petrol, my father used to walk the three miles there and back every day. Sometimes he'd persuade Flannagan, who worked in the garden for us, to collect him in the dog-cart in the evening, and always when he went to Dublin he arranged for Flannagan to meet the train he returned on. In the early hours of the morning I'd sometimes hear the rattle of the dog-cart on the avenue and then the wheels on the gravel outside the front of the house. At breakfast-time the next morning my father would say he was glad to be back again, and kiss my mother with the rest of us. The whole thing occurred once every month or so, the going away in the first place, the small packed suitcase in the hall, my father in his best tweed suit, Flannagan and the dog-cart. And the returning a few days later: breakfast with Mr. McNamara, my sister Charlotte used to say.

As a family we belonged to the past. We were Protestants in what had become Catholic Ireland. We'd once been part of an ascendancy, but now it was not so. Now there was the income from the granary and the mill, the house we lived in: we sold grain and flour, we wielded no power. 'Proddy-woddy green guts,' the Catholic children cried at us in Curransbridge. 'Catty, Catty, going to mass,' we whispered back, 'riding on the devil's ass.' They were as good as we were. It had not always been assumed so, and it sometimes seemed part of all the changing and the shifting of this and that, that Mr. McNamara, so honoured in our house, was a Catholic himself. 'A liberal, tolerant man,' my father used to say. 'No trace of the bigot in him.' In time, my father used to say, religious differences in Ireland wouldn't exist. The war would sort the whole matter out, even though as yet Ireland wasn't involved in it. When the war was over, and whether there was involvement or not, there wouldn't be any patience with religious differences. So, at least, Mr. McNamara appeared to argue.

Childhood was all that: my sisters, Charlotte, Amelia and Frances, and my parents gentle with each other, and Flannagan in the garden and Bridget our maid, and the avuncular spirit of Mr. McNamara. There was Miss Ryan as well, who arrived every morning on an old Raleigh bicycle, to teach the four of us, since the school at Curransbridge was not highly thought of by my parents. Miss Ryan had once been a nun.

The house itself was a Georgian rectangle when you looked straight at it, spaciously set against lawns which ran back to the curved brick of the kitchen-garden wall, with a gravel sweep in front, and an avenue running straight as a die for a mile and a half through fields where sheep grazed. My sisters had some world of their own which I knew I could not properly share. Charlotte, the oldest of them was five years younger that I was, Amelia was six and Frances five.

'Ah, he was in great form,' my father said on the morning of my thirteenth birthday. 'After a day listening to rubbish it's a pleasure to take a ball of malt with him.'

Frances giggled. When my father called a glass of whiskey a ball of malt Frances always giggled, and besides it was a giggly occasion. All my presents were sitting there on the sideboard, waiting for my father to finish his breakfast and to finish telling us about Mr. McNamara. But my father naturally took precedence: after all, he'd been away from the house for three days, he'd been cold and delayed on the train home, and attending to business in Dublin was something he disliked in any case. This time, though, as well as his business and the visit to Fleming's Hotel to see Mr. McNamara, I knew he'd bought the birthday present that he and my mother would jointly give me. Twenty minutes ago he'd walked into the dining-room with the wrapped parcel under his arm. 'Happy birthday, boy,' he'd said, placing the parcel on the sideboard beside the other three, from my sisters. It was the tradition in our house − a rule of my father's − that breakfast must be over and done with, every scrap eaten, before anyone opened a birthday present or a Christmas present.

'It was McNamara said that,' my father continued. 'Ivy-clad Ireland. It's the neutral condition of us.'

It was my father's opinion though not my mother's, that Ireland should have acceded to Winston Churchill's desire to man the Irish ports with English soldiers in case the Germans got in there first. Hitler had sent a telegram to de

Valera apologising for the accidental bombing of a creamery, which was a suspicious gesture in itself. Mr. McNamara, who also believed that de Valera should hand over the ports to Churchill, said that any gentlemanly gesture on the part of the German Führer was invariably followed by an act of savagery. Mr. McNamara, in spite of being a Catholic, was a keen admirer of the House of Windsor and of the English people. There was no aristocracy in the world to touch the English, he used to say, and no people, intent on elegance, succeeded as the English upper classes did. Class-consciousness in England was no bad thing, Mr. McNamara used to argue.

My father took from the side pocket of his jacket a small wrapped object. As he did so, my sisters rose from the breakfast table and marched to the sideboard. One by one my presents were placed before me, my parents' brought from the sideboard by my mother. It was a package about two and a half feet long, a few inches in width. It felt like a bundle of twigs and was in fact the various parts of a box-kite. Charlotte had bought me a book called *Dickon the Impossible*, Amelia a kaleidoscope. 'Open mine exceedingly carefully,' Frances said. I did, and at first I thought it was a pot of jam. It was a goldfish in a jar.

'From Mr. McNamara,' my father said, pointing at the smallest package. I'd forgotten it, because already the people who normally gave me presents were accounted for. 'I happened to mention,' my father said, 'that today was a certain day.'

It was so heavy that I thought it might be a lead soldier, or a horseman. In fact it was a dragon. It was tiny and complicated, and it appeared to be made of gold, but my father assured me it was brass. It had two green eyes that Frances said were emeralds and small pieces let into its back which she said looked like rubies. 'Priceless,' she whispered jealously. My father laughed and shook his head. The eyes and the pieces in the brass back were glass, he said.

I had never owned so beautiful an object. I watched it being passed from hand to hand around the breakfast table, impatient to feel it again myself. 'You must write at once to Mr. McNamara,' my mother said. 'It's far too generous of him,' she added, regarding my father with some slight disapproval, as though implying that my father shouldn't have accepted the gift. He vaguely shook his head, lighting a Sweet Afton. 'Give me the letter when you've done it.' he said. 'I have to go up again in a fortnight.'

I showed the dragon to Flannagan, who was thinning beetroot in the garden. I showed it to Bridget, our maid. 'Aren't you the lucky young hero?' Flannagan said, taking the dragon in a soil-caked hand. 'You'd get a five-pound note for that fellow, anywhere you cared to try.' Bridget polished it with Brasso for me.

That day I had a chocolate birthday cake, and sardine sandwiches, which were my favourite, and brown bread and greengage jam, a favourite also. After tea all the family watched while my father and I tried to fly the kite, running with it from one end of a lawn to the other. It was Flannagan who got it up for us in the end, and I remember the excitement of the string tugging at my fingers, and Bridget crying out that she'd never seen a thing like that before, wanting to know what it was for. 'Don't forget, dear, to write to Mr. McNamara first thing in the morning,' my mother reminded me when she kissed me goodnight. I wouldn't forget, I promised, and didn't add that of all my presents, including the beautiful green and yellow kite, I liked the dragon best.

But I never did write to Mr. McNamara. The next day was a different kind of day, a grim nightmare of a day during all of which someone in the house was weeping, and often several of us together. My father, so affectionate towards all of us, was no longer alive.

The war continued and Ireland continued to play no part in it. Further accidental German bombs were dropped and further apologies were sent to de Valera by the German Führer. Winston Churchill continued to fulminate about the ports, but the prophecy of Mr. McNamara that foreign soldiers would parade in O'Connell Street did not come true.

Knitting or sewing, my mother listened to the BBC news with a sadness in her eyes, unhappy that elsewhere death was occurring also. It was no help to any of us to be reminded that people in Britain and Europe were dying all the time now, with the same sudden awfulness as my father had.

Everything was different after my father died. My mother and I began to go for walks together. I'd take her arm, and sometimes her hand, knowing she was lonely. She talked about him to me, telling me about their honeymoon in Venice, the huge square where they'd sat drinking chocolate, listening to the bands that played there. She told me about my own birth, and how my father had given her a ring set with amber which he'd bought in Louis Wine's in Dublin. She would smile at me on our walks and tell me that even though I was only thirteen I was already taking his place. One day the house would be mine, she pointed out, and the mill and the granary. I'd marry, she said, and have children of my own, but I didn't want even to think about that. I didn't want to marry; I wanted my mother always to be there with me, going on walks and telling me about the person we all missed so much. We were still a family, my sisters and my mother and myself, Flannagan in the garden, and Bridget. I didn't want anything to change.

After the death of my father Mr. McNamara lived on, though in a different kind of way. The house in Palmerston Road, with Mr. McNamara's aunt drinking in an upstairs room, and the paper-thin Mrs. Matchette playing patience instead of being successful in the theatre, and Mr. Matchette with his squashed forehead, and Trixie O'Shea from Skibbereen, and the spaniel called Wolfe Tone: all of them remained quite vividly alive after my father's death, as part of our memory of him. Fleming's Hotel remained also, and all the talk there'd been there of the eccentric household in Palmerston Road. For almost as long as I could remember, and certainly as long as my sisters could remember, our own household had regularly been invaded by the other one, and after my father's death my sisters and I often recalled specific incidents retailed in Fleming's Hotel and later at our breakfast table. There'd been the time when Mr McNamara's aunt had sold the house to a man she met outside a public house. And the time when Mrs. Matchette appeared to have fallen in love with Garda Molloy, who used to call in at the kitchen for Trixie O'Shea every night. And the time the spaniel was run over by a van and didn't die. All of it was preserved, with Mr. McNamara himself, white-haired and portly in the smoke-brown bar of Fleming's Hotel, where snuff could be bought, and Bovril as well as whiskey.

A few months after the death my mother remarked one breakfast-time that no doubt Mr. McNamara had seen the obituary notice in the *Irish Times*. 'Oh, but you should write,' my sister Frances cried out in her excitable manner. My mother shook her head. My father and Mr. McNamara had been bar-room friends, she pointed out: letters in either direction would not be in order. Charlotte and Amelia agreed with this opinion, but Frances still protested. I couldn't see that it mattered. 'He gave us all that chocolate,' Frances cried, 'and the biscuits.' My mother said again that Mr. McNamara was not the kind of man to write to about a death, nor the kind who would write himself. The letter that I was to have written thanking him for the dragon was not mentioned. Disliking the writing of letters, I didn't raise the subject myself.

At the end of that year I was sent to a boarding-school in the Dublin mountains. Miss Ryan continued to come to the house on her Raleigh to teach my sisters, and I'd have far preferred to have remained at home with her. It could not be: the boarding-school in the Dublin mountains, a renowned Protestant monument, had been my father's chosen destiny for me and that was that. If he hadn't died, leaving home might perhaps have been more painful, but the death had brought with it practical complications and

167

troubles, mainly concerned with the running of the granary and the mill: going away to school was slight compared with all that or so my mother convinced me.

The headmaster of the renowned school was a small, red-skinned English cleric. With other new boys, I had tea with him and his wife in the drawing-room some days after term began. We ate small ham-paste sandwiches and Battenburg cake. The headmaster's wife, a cold woman in grey, asked me what I intended to do — 'in life', as she put it. I said I'd run a granary and a mill at Curransbridge; she didn't seem interested. The headmaster told us he was in *Who's Who*. Otherwise the talk was of the war.

Miss Ryan had not prepared me well. 'Dear boy, whoever taught you French?' a man with a pipe asked me, and did not stay to hear my answer. 'Your Latin, really!' another man exclaimed, and the man who taught me mathematics warned me never to set my sights on a profession that involved an understanding of figures. I sat in the back row of the class with other boys who had been ill-prepared for the renowned school.

I don't know when it was — a year, perhaps, or eighteen months after my first term — that I developed an inquisitiveness about my father. Had he, I wondered, been as bad at everything as I was? Had some other man with a pipe scorned his inadequacy when it came to French? Had he felt, as I did, a kind of desperation when faced with algebra? You'd *have* to know a bit about figures, I used, almost miserably, to say to myself: you'd have to if you hoped to run a granary and a mill. Had he been good at mathematics?

I asked my mother these questions, and other questions like them. But my mother was vague in her replies and said she believed, although perhaps she was wrong, that my father had not been good at mathematics. She laughed when I asked the questions. She told me to do my best.

But the more I thought about the future, and about myself in terms of the man whose place I was to take, the more curious I became about him. In the holidays my mother and I still went on our walks together, through the garden and then into the fields that stretched behind it, along the banks of the river that flowed through Curransbridge. But my mother spoke less and less about my father because increasingly there was less to say, except with repetition. I imagined the huge square in Venice and the cathedral and the bands playing outside the cafés. I imagined hundreds of other scenes, her own varied memories of their relationship and their marriage. We often walked in silence now, or I talked more myself, drawing her into a world of cross-country runs, and odorous changing-rooms, and the small headmaster's repeated claim that the food we ate had a high calorific value. School was ordinarily dreary: I told her how we smoked wartime American cigarettes in mud huts specially constructed for the purpose and how we relished the bizarre when, now and again, it broke the monotony. There was a master called Mr. Dingle, whose practice it was to enquire of new boys the colour and nature of their mother's night-dresses. In the oak-panelled dining-hall that smelt of mince and the butter that generations had flicked on to the ceiling, Mr. Dingle's eye would glaze as he sat at the end of a Junior House table while one boy after another fuelled him with the stuff of fantasies. On occasions when parents visited the school he would observe through cigarette smoke the mothers of these new boys, stripping them of their skirts and blouses in favour of the night clothes that their sons had described for him. There was another master, known as Buller Achen, who was reputed to take a sensual interest in the sheep that roamed the mountainsides, and a boy called Testane-Hackett who was possessed of the conviction that he was the second son of God. In the dining-hall a gaunt black-clad figure, a butler called Tripp, hovered about the high table where sat the headmaster and the prefects assisted by a maid, said to be his daughter, who was known to us as the Bicycle. There was Fisher Major, who never washed, and Strapping, who disastrously attempted to treat some kind of foot ailment with mild acid. My mother listened appreciatively, and I often saw in her eyes the same look that had been there at breakfast-time when my father spoke of Fleming's Hotel and Mr. McNamara. 'How like him you are!' she now and again murmured, smiling at me.

At Curransbridge I stood in his office above the mill, a tiny room now occupied by the man my mother had chosen to look after things, a Mr. Devereux. In the house I rooted through the belongings he'd left behind; I stared at photographs of him. With Flannagan and my sisters I flew the kite he'd bought me that last time he'd been to Dublin. I polished the small brass dragon that his bar-room companion had given him to give to me. 'It's the boy's birthday,' I imagined him saying in the brown bar of Fleming's Hotel, and I imagined the slow movement of Mr. McNamara's hand as he drew the dragon from his pocket. It was inevitable, I suppose, that sooner or later I should seek out Fleming's Hotel.

'An uncle,' I said to the small headmaster. 'Passing through Dublin, sir.'

'Passing? Passing? He had a Home Counties accent and a hard nasal intonation. 'Passing?' he said again, giving the word an extra vowel sound.

'On his way to Galway, sir. He's in the R.A.F., sir. I think he'd like to see me, sir, because my father —'

'Ah, yes, yes. Back in time for Chapel, please.'

Fleming's Hotel, it said in the telephone directory, *21 Wheeler Street.* As I cycled down from the mountains, I didn't know what I was going to do when I got there.

It was a narrow, four-storey building in a terrace with others, a bleak-looking grey stone facade. The white woodwork of the windows needed a coat of paint, the glass portico over the entrance doors had a dusty look. It was on this dusty glass that the name Fleming's Hotel was picked out in white enamel letters stuck to the glass itself. I cycled past the hotel twice, glancing at the windows — a dozen of them, the four at the top much smaller than the others — and at the entrance doors. No one left or entered. I propped the bicycle against the edge of the pavement some distance away from the hotel, outside what seemed to be the street's only shop, a green-grocer's. There were pears in the window. I went in and bought one.

I wheeled the bicycle away from the shop and came, at the end of the street, to a canal. Slowly I ate the pear, and then I took my red and green school cap from my head and wheeled my bicycle slowly back to Fleming's Hotel. I pushed open one of the entrance doors and for a split second I heard my father's voice again, describing what I now saw: the smokiness of the low-ceilinged hall, a coal fire burning, and a high reception counter with the hotel's register open on it, and a brass bell beside the register. There were brown leather armchairs in the hall and a brown leather bench running along one wall. Gas lamps were lit but even so, and in spite of the fact that it was four o'clock in the afternoon, the hall was dim. It was empty of other people and quiet. A tall grandfather clock ticked, the fire occasionally hissed. There was a smell of some kind of soup. It was the nicest, most comfortable hall I'd even been in.

Beyond it, I could see another coal fire, through an archway. That was the bar where they used to sit, where for all I knew Mr. McNamara was sitting now. I imagined my father crossing the hall as I crossed it myself. The bar was the same as the hall, with the same kind of leather chairs, and a leather bench and gas lamps and a low ceiling. There were net curtains pulled across the two windows, and one wall was taken up with a counter, with bottles on shelves behind it, and leather-topped stools in front of it. There was a woman sitting by the fire drinking orange-coloured liquid from a small glass. Behind the bar a man in a white jacket was reading the *Irish Independent*.

I paused in the archway that divided the bar from the hall. I was under age. I had no right to take a further step and I didn't know what to do or to say if I did. I didn't know what drink to order. I didn't know if in the dim gaslight I looked a child.

I went to the bar and stood there. The man didn't look up from his newspaper. *Smithwick's Ale* were words on the labels of bottles. I would ask for a Smithwick's Ale. All I wanted was to be allowed to remain, to sit down with the beer and to think about my father. If Mr. McNamara did not come today he'd come another day. Francis had been right: he should have been written to. I should have written to him myself, to thank my father's friend for his present.

'Good evening,' the barman said.

'Smithwick's, please,' I said as casually as I could. Not knowing how much the drink might be, I placed a ten-shilling note on the bar.

'Drop of lime in it, sir?

'Lime? Oh, yes. Yes, please. Thanks very much.'

'Choppy kind of day,' the barman said.

I took the glass and my change, and sat dawn as far as possible from where the woman was sitting. I sat so that I was facing both the bar and the archway, so that if Mr. McNamara came in I'd see him at once. I'd have to leave at six o'clock in order to be safely back for Chapel at seven.

I finished the beer. I took an envelope out of my pocket and drew pieces of holly on the back of it, a simple art-form that Miss Ryan had taught all of us. I took my glass to the bar and asked for another Smithwick's. The barman had a pale, unhealthy-seeming face, and wire-rimmed glasses, and a very thin neck. 'You do want the best, don't you?' he said in a joky kind of voice, imitating someone. 'Bird's Custard,' he said in the same joky way, 'and Bird's Jelly de Luxe.' My father had mentioned this barman: he was repeating the advertisements of Radio Éireann. 'You do want the best, don't you?' he said again, pushing the glass of beer towards me. By the fire, the woman made a noise, a slight, tired titter of amusement. I laughed myself, politely too.

When I returned to my armchair I found the woman was looking at me. I wondered if she could be a prostitute, alone in a hotel bar like that. A boy at school called Yeats claimed that prostitutes hung around railway stations mostly, and on quays. But there was of course no reason why you shouldn't come across one in a bar.

Yet she seemed too quietly-dressed to be a prostitute. She was wearing a green suit and a green hat, and there was a coat made of some kind of fur draped over a chair near the chair she sat on. She was a dark-haired woman with an oval face. I'd no idea what age she was: somewhere between thirty and forty, I imagined: I wasn't good at guessing people's ages.

The Smithwick's Ale was having an effect on me. I wanted to giggle. How extraordinary it would be, I thought, if a prostitute tried to sell herself to me in my father's and Mr. McNamara's hotel. After all, there was no reason at all why some prostitutes shouldn't be quietly-dressed, probably the more expensive ones were. I could feel myself smiling, holding back the giggle. Naturally enough, I thought, my father hadn't mentioned the presence of prostitutes in Fleming's Hotel. And then I thought that perhaps, if he'd lived, he would have told me one day, when my sisters and my mother weren't in the room. It was the kind of thing, surely, that fathers did tell sons.

I took the envelope I'd drawn the holly on out of my pocket and read the letter it contained. They were managing, my mother said. Miss Ryan had had a dose of flu, Charlotte and Amelia wanted to breed horses, Frances didn't know what she wanted to do. His rheumatics were slowing Flannagan down a bit in the garden. Bridget was insisting on cleaning the drawing-room chimney. *It'll be lovely at Christmas*, she wrote. *So nice being all together again*.

The oval-faced woman put on her fur coat, and on her way from the bar she passed close to where I was sitting. She looked down and smiled at me.

'Hills of the North, rejoice!' we sang in chapel that night. 'Valley and lowland, sing!'

I smelt of Smithwick's Ale. I knew I did because as we'd stood in line in Cloisters several other boys had remarked on it. As I sang, I knew I was puffing the smell all over everyone else. 'Like a bloody brewery,' Gahan Minor said afterwards.

'. . . this night,' intoned the small headmaster nasally, 'and for ever more.'

'Amen,' we all replied.

Saturday night was a pleasant time. After Chapel there were two and a half hours during which you could do more or less what you liked, provided the master on duty knew where you were. You could work in the Printing Shop or read in the Library, or take part in a debate, such as that this school is an outpost of the British Empire, or play billiards or do carpentry, or go to the model railway club or the music-rooms. At half-past nine there was some even freer time, during which the master on duty didn't have to know where you were. Most boys went for a smoke then.

After Chapel on the Saturday night after I'd visited Fleming's Hotel I read in the Library. I read *Jane Eyre*, but all the time the oval face of the woman in the hotel kept appearing in my mind. It would stay there for a few seconds and then fade, and then return. Again and again, as I read *Jane Eyre*, she passed close to my chair in the bar of Fleming's Hotel, and looked down and smiled at me.

The end of that term came. The Sixth Form and Remove did *Macbeth* on the last two nights, A. McC. P. Jackson giving what was generally regarded as a fine performance as Banquo. Someone stole the secondhand Penguin I'd bought from Grace Major to read on the train, *Why didn't They Ask Evans?* Aitcheson and Montgomery were found conversing in the shower-room in the middle of the night.

On the journey home I was unable to stop thinking about Fleming's Hotel. A man in the carriage lent me a copy of *Barrack Variety*, but the jokes didn't seem funny. It was at moments like these that the truth most harshly mocked me. Ever since I'd found the hotel, ever since the woman had stared at me, it had been a part of every day, and for whole nights in my long, cheerless dormitory I had been unable to sleep. My father's voice had returned to me there, telling again the stories of his friend, and reminding me of his friend's opinions. My father had disagreed with my mother in her view that de Valera should not hand over the ports to Churchill, preferring to share the view of his friend. At school and on the train, and most of all when I returned home, the truth made me feel ill, as though I had the flu.

That Christmas morning we handed each other our presents, after we'd eaten, still observing my father's rule. We thought of him then, they in one way, I in another. 'Oh, my dear, how lovely!' my mother whispered over some ornament I'd bought her in a Dublin shop. I had thrown the dragon with the green glass eyes far into a lake near the school, unable to understand how my father had ever brought it to the house, or brought bars of chocolate or tins of Jacob's biscuits. To pass to his children beneath my mother's eyes the gifts of another woman seemed as awful a sin as any father could commit, yet somehow it was not as great as the sin of sharing with all of us this other woman's eccentric household, her sister and her sister's husband, her alcoholic aunt, a maid and a dog. 'That's Norah McNamara,' the barman's voice seemed to say again at our breakfast table, and I imagined them sitting there, my father and she, in that comfortable bar, and my father listening to her talk of the house in Palmerston Road and of how she admired the English aristocracy. I watched my mother smile that Christmas morning, and I wanted to tell the truth because the truth was neat and without hypocrisy: I wanted carefully to say that I was glad my father was dead.

Instead I left the breakfast table and went to my bedroom. I wept there, and then washed my face in cold water from the jug on my wash-stand. I hated the memory of him and how he would have been that Christmas morning; I hated him for destroying everything. It was no consolation to me then that he had tried to share with us a person he loved in a way that was different from the way he loved us. I could neither forgive nor understand. I felt only bitterness that I, who had taken his place, must now continue his deception, and keep the secret of his lies and his hypocrisy.